EVIL EMPEROR PENGUIN STRIKES BACK!

LAURA ELLEN ANDERSON

dfb David Fickling Books
the PHOENIX
SCHOLASTIC

FRIDGE OF EVIL
OS-EVIL
PENGUIN EDITION
THE HUGENATOR
X+1= Penguin / Big = HUGE
STAND HERE
10 SECS
TRIGGER BUTTON LOOKS LIKE PAINT!
ME
ZZZZAP!
WORLD LEADER
TURNED INTO A PAINTING!
BRAINY
MAKES LOVELY CUPS OF TEA
REALLY KIND
MISTER 8
WANTS TO TAKE OVER THE WORLD
LOVES SPAGHETTI RINGS
SCARED OF HIS MOM
EVIL MASTER
TOP MINION
LOVES HAPPY THINGS
EUGENE (THAT'S ME!)
LOVELY
FLIES USING RAINBOWS
MY BEST FRIEND
KEITH!
ARCH-NEMESIS!
ALSO WANTS TO TAKE OVER THE WORLD
NOT VERY NICE!
EVIL CAT
FOR "THE LEAGUE"... A TOP-NOTCH BUNCH OF LOVELIES!
THE DASTARDLY DANNY
THE LUXURIOUS LUKE
THE KINDHEARTED KAYLEIGH
THE REMARKABLE RITCHIE
LOVE YOU GUYS!

PAGE	EPISODE

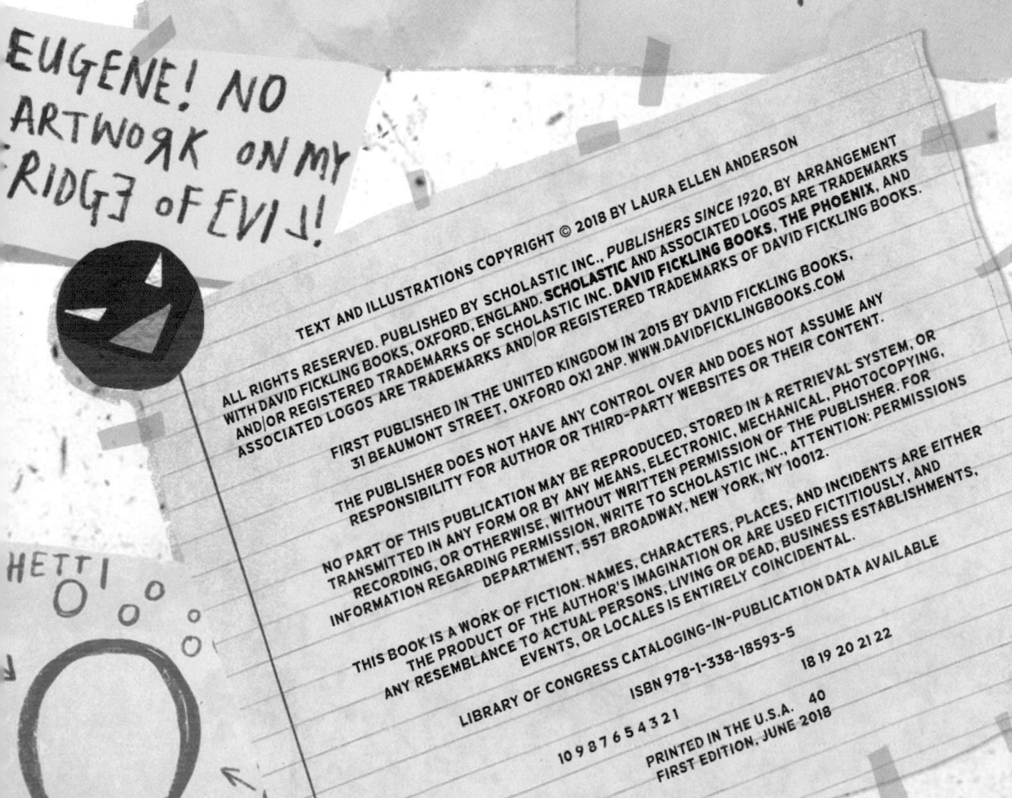

 PUBLISHED BY SCHOLASTIC INC., *PUBLISHERS SINCE 1920*, BY ARRANGEMENT WITH DAVID FICKLING BOOKS, OXFORD, ENGLAND. **SCHOLASTIC** AND ASSOCIATED LOGOS ARE TRADEMARKS AND/OR REGISTERED TRADEMARKS OF SCHOLASTIC INC. **DAVID FICKLING BOOKS, THE PHOENIX**, AND ASSOCIATED LOGOS ARE TRADEMARKS AND/OR REGISTERED TRADEMARKS OF DAVID FICKLING BOOKS.

FIRST PUBLISHED IN THE UNITED KINGDOM IN 2015 BY DAVID FICKLING BOOKS, 31 BEAUMONT STREET, OXFORD OX1 2NP. WWW.DAVIDFICKLINGBOOKS.COM

LIBRARY OF CONGRESS CATALOGING-IN-PUBLICATION DATA AVAILABLE

ISBN 978-1-338-18593-5

10 9 8 7 6 5 4 3 2 1 18 19 20 21 22

PRINTED IN THE U.S.A. 40
FIRST EDITION, JUNE 2018

I WILL BURP YOU: PART 1
DINNER WILL BE READY IN FIVE MINUTES, SIR...
OH, WILL IT NOW?
ERR... YES, SIR.
WE'LL SEE, NUMBER 8, WE'LL SEE...
EUGENE, TURN UP THE HEAT...
THE "YOUTH JUICE" IS ENTERING ITS FINAL STAGE OF COMPLETION.
HOT
VERY HOT
JUST RIGHT
THEN IT'S READY?
YEEEESSSSS, IT SHALL BE READY.
I DO BELIEVE THE "DE-AGEFIER" IS MY FINEST INVENTION YET!
HOW DOES IT WORK?
WELL, THE "DE-AGEFIER" RUNS ON MY PATENTED "YOUTH JUICE."
ONCE READY, THE "YOUTH JUICE" HAS THE ABILITY TO TURN A FULLY GROWN HUMAN BACK INTO THEIR BABY FORM.
THE "YOUTH JUICE" WILL BE STORED IN THESE CANISTERS THAT CAN BE STRAPPED TO YOUR BACK LIKE A BACKPACK...
DE-AGEFIER
STRAPS
BLUE PRINT
HOSE
Trigger
Firing Snout
ME
Body Clock
WHEN YOU PULL THE TRIGGER, THE "DE-AGEFIER" POWER PACK FIRES UP, TURNING BACK THE BODY-CLOCK METER.
THEN BLAST 'EM!
THE LONGER YOU SHOOT THE "YOUTH JUICE" AT A HUMAN, THE YOUNGER THEY GET!
ONCE I TURN THE WORLD INTO USE-LESS BABIES, I WILL RULE THEM ALL!
DINNER'S READY!
ARGH! NUMBER 8, YOU'RE RUINING THE MOST EVIL PART OF MY PLAN!

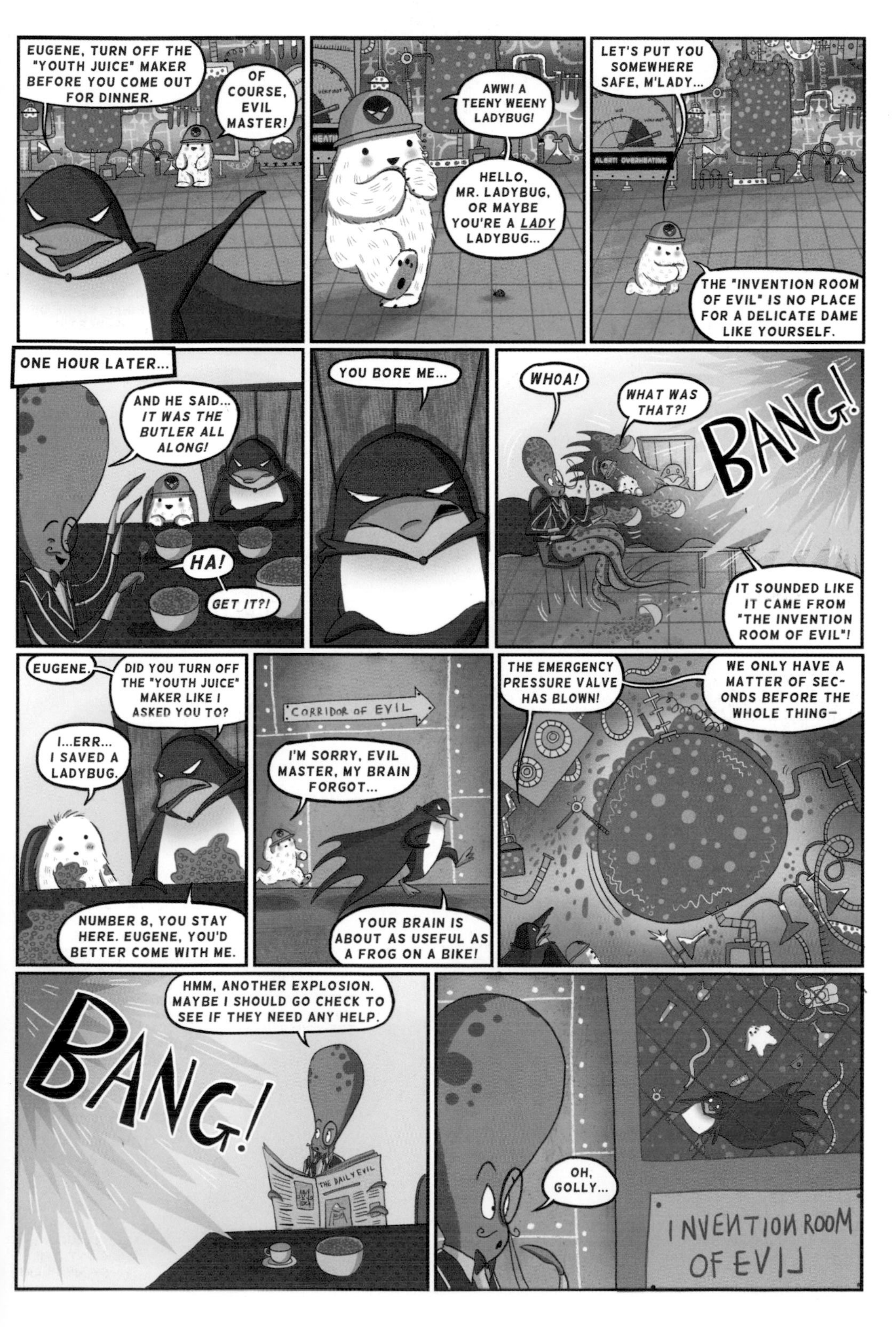
EUGENE, TURN OFF THE "YOUTH JUICE" MAKER BEFORE YOU COME OUT FOR DINNER.
OF COURSE, EVIL MASTER!
AWW! A TEENY WEENY LADYBUG!
HELLO, MR. LADYBUG, OR MAYBE YOU'RE A LADY LADYBUG...
LET'S PUT YOU SOMEWHERE SAFE, M'LADY...
ALERT! OVERHEATING
THE "INVENTION ROOM OF EVIL" IS NO PLACE FOR A DELICATE DAME LIKE YOURSELF.
ONE HOUR LATER...
AND HE SAID... IT WAS THE BUTLER ALL ALONG!
HA!
GET IT?!
YOU BORE ME...
WHOA!
WHAT WAS THAT?!
BANG!
IT SOUNDED LIKE IT CAME FROM "THE INVENTION ROOM OF EVIL"!
EUGENE.
DID YOU TURN OFF THE "YOUTH JUICE" MAKER LIKE I ASKED YOU TO?
I...ERR... I SAVED A LADYBUG.
NUMBER 8, YOU STAY HERE. EUGENE, YOU'D BETTER COME WITH ME.
CORRIDOR OF EVIL
I'M SORRY, EVIL MASTER, MY BRAIN FORGOT...
YOUR BRAIN IS ABOUT AS USEFUL AS A FROG ON A BIKE!
THE EMERGENCY PRESSURE VALVE HAS BLOWN!
WE ONLY HAVE A MATTER OF SEC-ONDS BEFORE THE WHOLE THING—
BANG!
HMM, ANOTHER EXPLOSION. MAYBE I SHOULD GO CHECK TO SEE IF THEY NEED ANY HELP.
THE DAILY EVIL
OH, GOLLY...
INVENTION ROOM OF EVIL

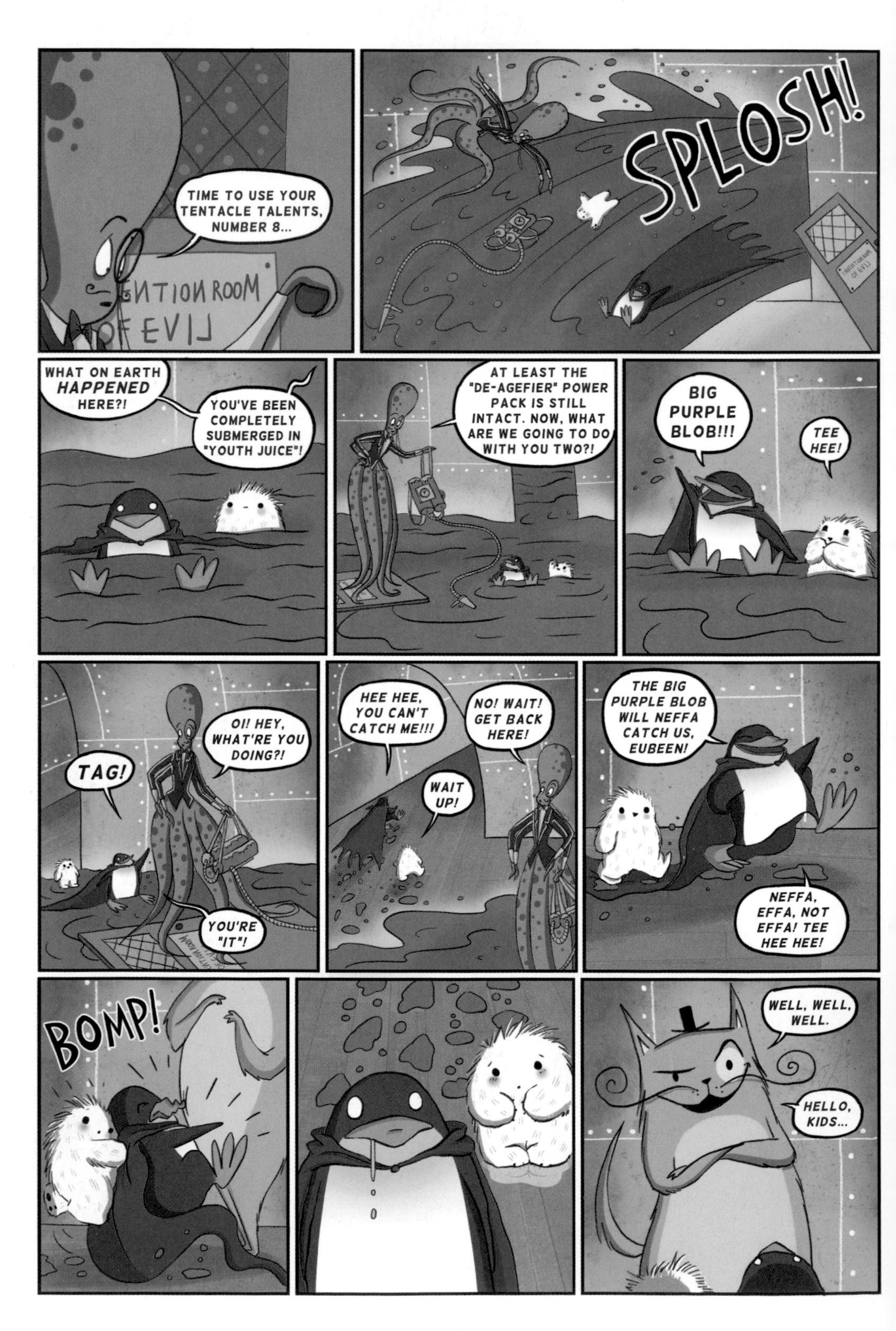
TIME TO USE YOUR TENTACLE TALENTS, NUMBER 8...
SPLOSH!
WHAT ON EARTH HAPPENED HERE?!
YOU'VE BEEN COMPLETELY SUBMERGED IN "YOUTH JUICE"!
AT LEAST THE "DE-AGEFIER" POWER PACK IS STILL INTACT. NOW, WHAT ARE WE GOING TO DO WITH YOU TWO?!
BIG PURPLE BLOB!!!
TEE HEE!
OI! HEY, WHAT'RE YOU DOING?!
TAG!
YOU'RE "IT"!
HEE HEE, YOU CAN'T CATCH ME!!!
NO! WAIT! GET BACK HERE!
WAIT UP!
THE BIG PURPLE BLOB WILL NEFFA CATCH US, EUBEEN!
NEFFA, EFFA, NOT EFFA! TEE HEE HEE!
BOMP!
WELL, WELL, WELL.
HELLO, KIDS...

I WILL BURP YOU: PART 2

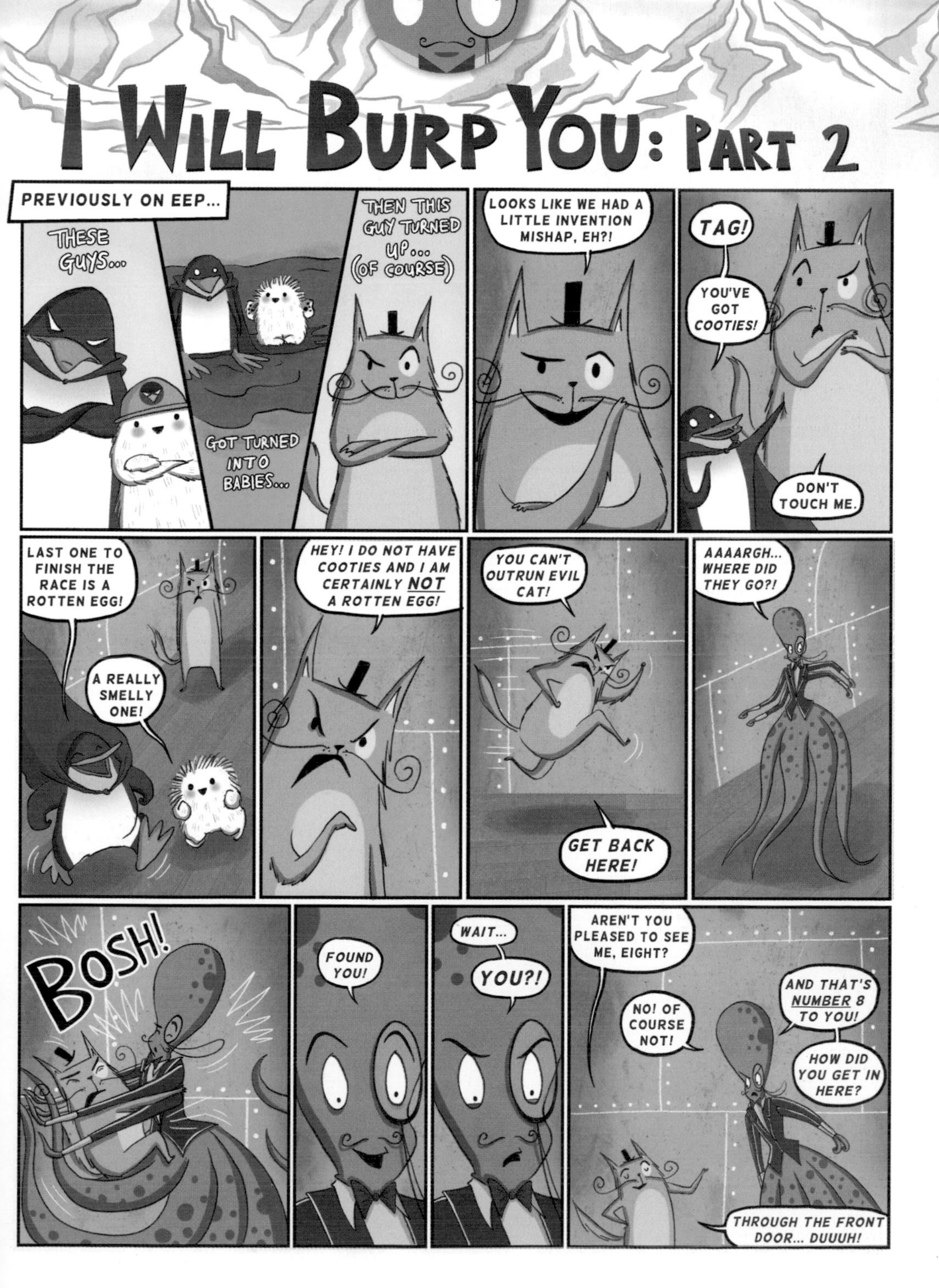

AND JUST TO SPITE YOU, I DIDN'T CLOSE THE DOOR BEHIND ME.
OH NO...
UH, HELLO?! RUUUDE!
THIS IS GOING TO BE LIKE TRYING TO FIND A NEEDLE IN A HAY-STACK...
EXCEPT IT'S A SMALL WHITE MINION IN ANTARCTICA.
EUGEEEENE!
HMMM, I KNOW...
I MADE EXTRA SPAGHETTI RINGS AND CHOCOLATE BUTTONS FOR DESSERT!
OOO!
GOTCHA!
I GOT CATCHED!
OKAY, EUGENE, YOU NEED TO TELL ME WHERE YOUR EVIL MASTER IS...
I LIKE YOU.
RIGHT HERE!
MWAHAHAHAAAR!
GIVE ME BACK THE PENGUIN!
WHAT USE IS HE TO YOU NOW?! HE'S ALL SMALL AND USELESS...
THEN AGAIN, NOT MUCH HAS CHANGED.
DON'T YOU DARE INSULT EVIL EMPEROR PENGUIN!
NER NER!
NUMBER 8 IS A ROTTEN EGG AND HE'S GOT COOTIES!
OH, I REMEMBERED TO CLOSE THE DOOR THIS TIME!
SAY GOOD-BYE TO YOUR LITTLE PENGUIN!
OPEN UP, CAT!
I NEED TO PEE.
CORRIDOR OF EVIL
Y'KNOW, WE COULD HAVE BEEN THE ULTIMATE EVIL TEAM...
BUT YOU'D CRAMP MY STYLE.
NOW I MUST DESTROY YOU.
MEANWHILE...
ARGH, IT'S NO USE... THE "CHUBB LOCK OF EVIL" IS TOO STRONG.
EUGENE, WHAT AM I GOING TO DO?!

EUGENE, GIVE BACK THE MONOCLE. IT MAKES ME LOOK IMPORTANT.
MONOCLE!
EUGENE! YOU'RE A GENIUS!
I CAN SLIDE THE LOCK OPEN WITH IT!
YES! IT'S WORKING!
LET'S GET OUR EVIL MASTER BACK!
I'M PEEING!
SO, THIS WAS YOUR LATEST PLAN THEN, EH?!
THIS INFORMS ME THAT THE LONGER I BLAST SOMEONE WITH THIS THING, THE YOUNGER THEY GET.
SO SURELY, IF I BLAST YOU... YOU'LL NO LONGER EXIST!
I'M SURE THERE'S JUST ENOUGH JUICE IN HERE TO FINISH YOU OFF...
NOW HOW DOES THIS THING WORK...?
I KNOW EXACTLY WHERE THAT RAT OF A CAT WILL BE!
CAT!
SAY GOOD-BYE TO YOUR EXISTENCE, TINY BIRD!
CLICK
NOOOOOOO!
SPLAT!
MEW.
WELL, WHADDAYA KNOW! THE "DE-AGEFIER" DIDN'T WORK PROPERLY ANYWAY.
WHO'D HAVE THOUGHT, SIR, THAT YOUR FAILED ATTEMPT AT WORLD DOMINATION WOULD SAVE YOUR LIFE!
NOW, I JUST NEED TO FIGURE OUT A PLAN TO CHANGE YOU BACK...
I WANNA PULL THE KITTY'S WHISKERS!
THIS WAS EASIER SAID THAN DONE...
I WANNA HUG HIM FOREVER!
PLAN

HUGENE
WHAT A GLORIOUSLY EVIL DAY!
WARDROBE OF EVIL
AWESOME STUFF
HMMM, WHAT TO WEAR, WHAT TO WEAR?
GOOD MORNING, SIR. YOU'RE AWFULLY CHIPPER TODAY.
YOU HAVEN'T EVEN INSULTED ME YET...
WELL, MY JOLLY OL' SEAL...
IT'S OCTO– D'YOU KNOW WHAT, NEVER MIND.
I'VE HAD THE BEST WORLD DOMINATION IDEA! IT CAME TO ME IN A DREEEEAM!
I DREAMED I WAS HUGE, NUMBER 8. HUGE AND MUSCLY! EVERYONE OBEYED ME BECAUSE THEY WERE TOO TERRIFIED NOT TO!
I WOKE UP AND REALIZED THIS DREAM COULD BE A REALITY!
I SHALL INVENT A DEVICE TO MAKE ME THE BIGGEST PENGUIN YOU'VE EVER SEEN!
I'VE WRITTEN DOWN THE NECESSARY CALCULATIONS. I JUST NEED YOU TO DO ALL THE HARD WORK.
THE HUGENATOR
X+1= Penguin / Big = HUGE
10 SECS
STAND HERE
NO TIME FOR TEA, NUMBER 8. YOU'D BETTER GET CRACKING! I HAVE A WORLD TO TAKE OVER.

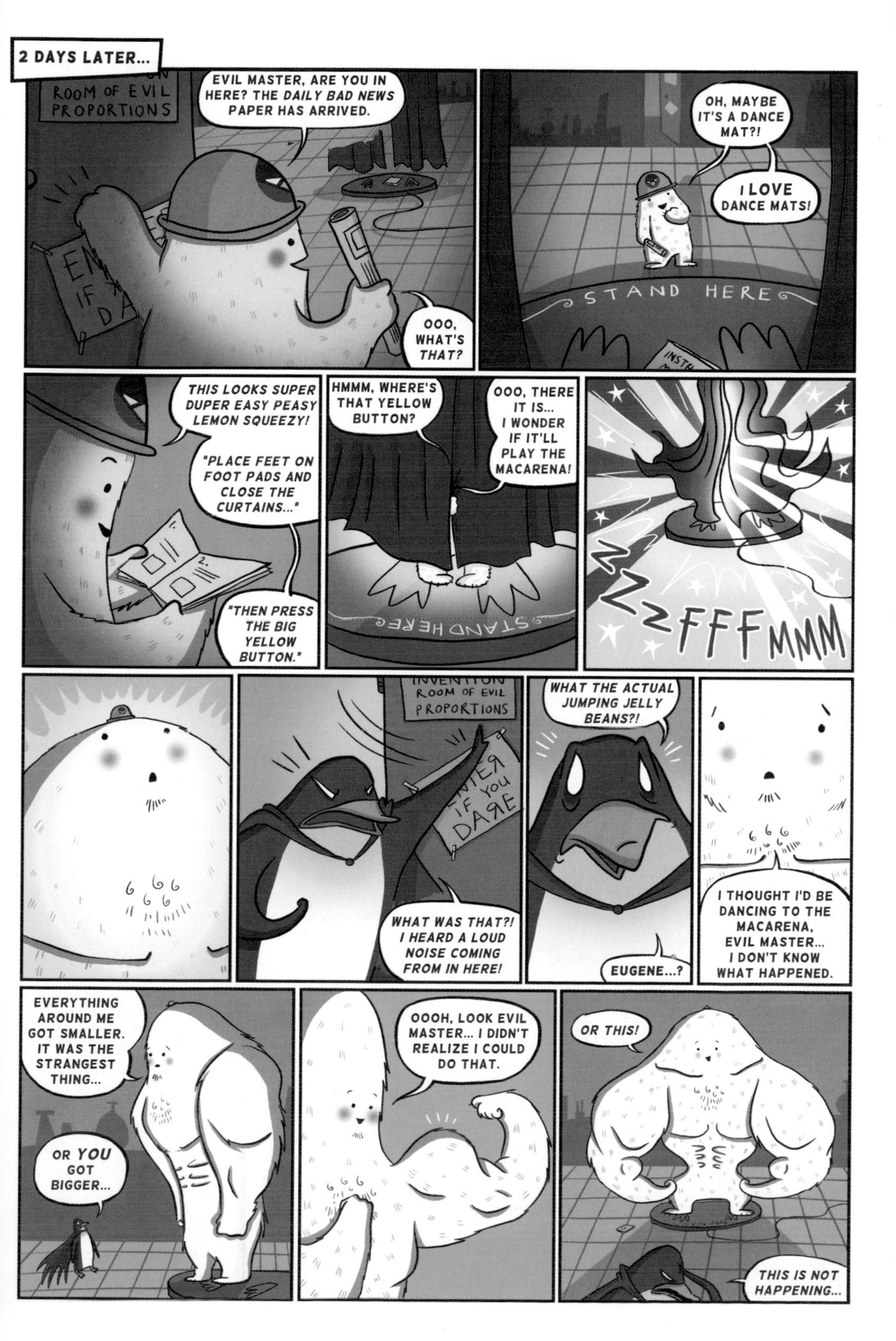
2 DAYS LATER...
ROOM OF EVIL PROPORTIONS
EVIL MASTER, ARE YOU IN HERE? THE *DAILY BAD NEWS* PAPER HAS ARRIVED.
OOO, WHAT'S *THAT?*
OH, MAYBE IT'S A DANCE MAT?!
I LOVE DANCE MATS!
STAND HERE
THIS LOOKS SUPER DUPER EASY PEASY LEMON SQUEEZY!
"PLACE FEET ON FOOT PADS AND CLOSE THE CURTAINS..."
"THEN PRESS THE BIG YELLOW BUTTON."
HMMM, WHERE'S THAT YELLOW BUTTON?
OOO, THERE IT IS... I WONDER IF IT'LL PLAY THE MACARENA!
STAND HERE
ZZZFFFMMM
ROOM OF EVIL PROPORTIONS
ENTER IF YOU DARE
WHAT WAS THAT?! I HEARD A LOUD NOISE COMING FROM IN HERE!
WHAT THE ACTUAL JUMPING JELLY BEANS?!
EUGENE...?
I THOUGHT I'D BE DANCING TO THE MACARENA, EVIL MASTER... I DON'T KNOW WHAT HAPPENED.
EVERYTHING AROUND ME GOT SMALLER. IT WAS THE STRANGEST THING...
OR *YOU* GOT BIGGER...
OOOH, LOOK EVIL MASTER... I DIDN'T REALIZE I COULD DO THAT.
OR THIS!
THIS IS NOT HAPPENING...

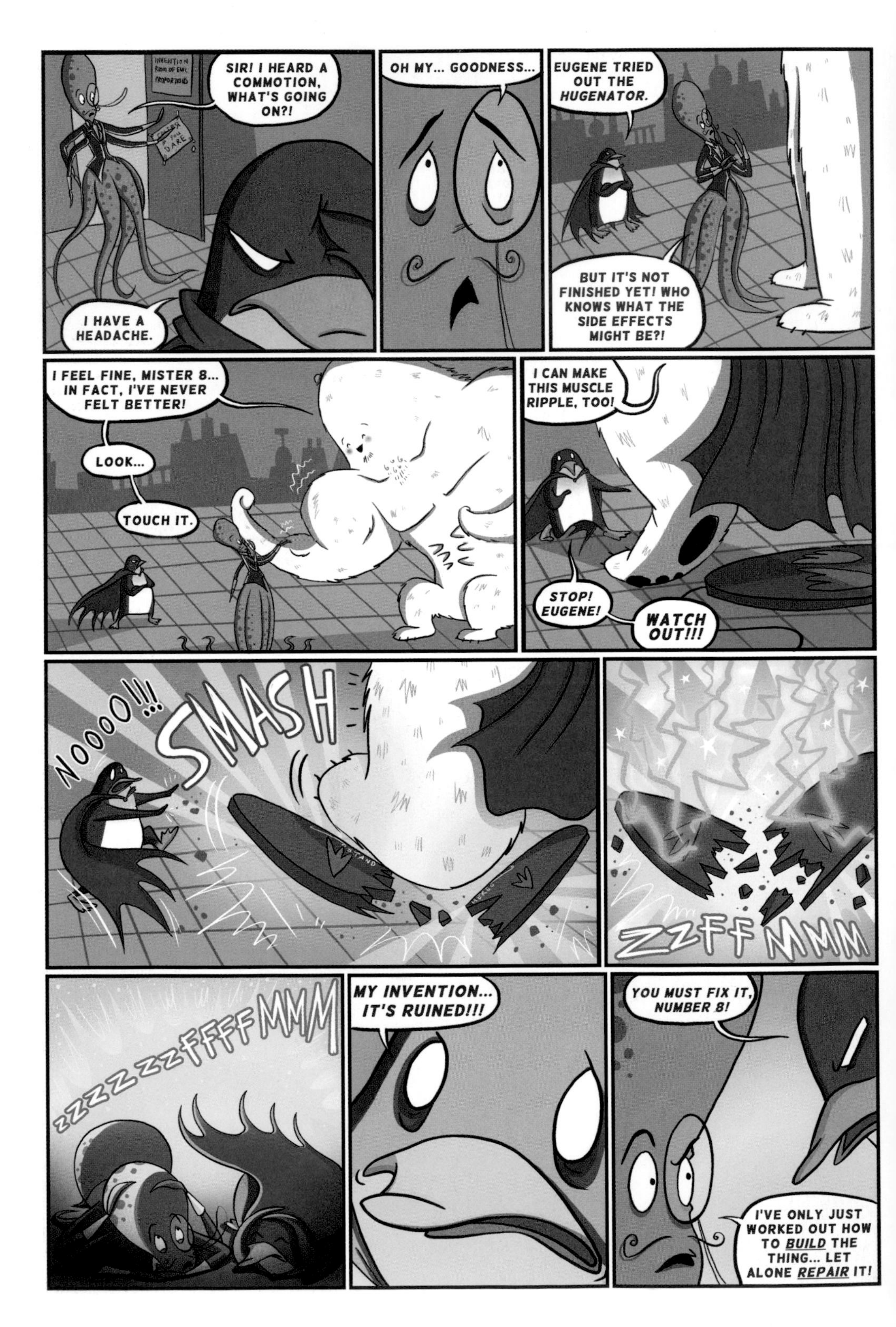
SIR! I HEARD A COMMOTION, WHAT'S GOING ON?!
I HAVE A HEADACHE.
OH MY... GOODNESS...
EUGENE TRIED OUT THE *HUGENATOR*.
BUT IT'S NOT FINISHED YET! WHO KNOWS WHAT THE SIDE EFFECTS MIGHT BE?!
I FEEL FINE, MISTER 8... IN FACT, I'VE NEVER FELT BETTER!
LOOK...
TOUCH IT.
I CAN MAKE THIS MUSCLE RIPPLE, TOO!
STOP! EUGENE!
WATCH OUT!!!
NOOOO!!!
SMASH
ZZFF MMM
ZZZZZZFFFF MMM
MY INVENTION... IT'S RUINED!!!
YOU MUST FIX IT, NUMBER 8!
I'VE ONLY JUST WORKED OUT HOW TO *BUILD* THE THING... LET ALONE *REPAIR* IT!

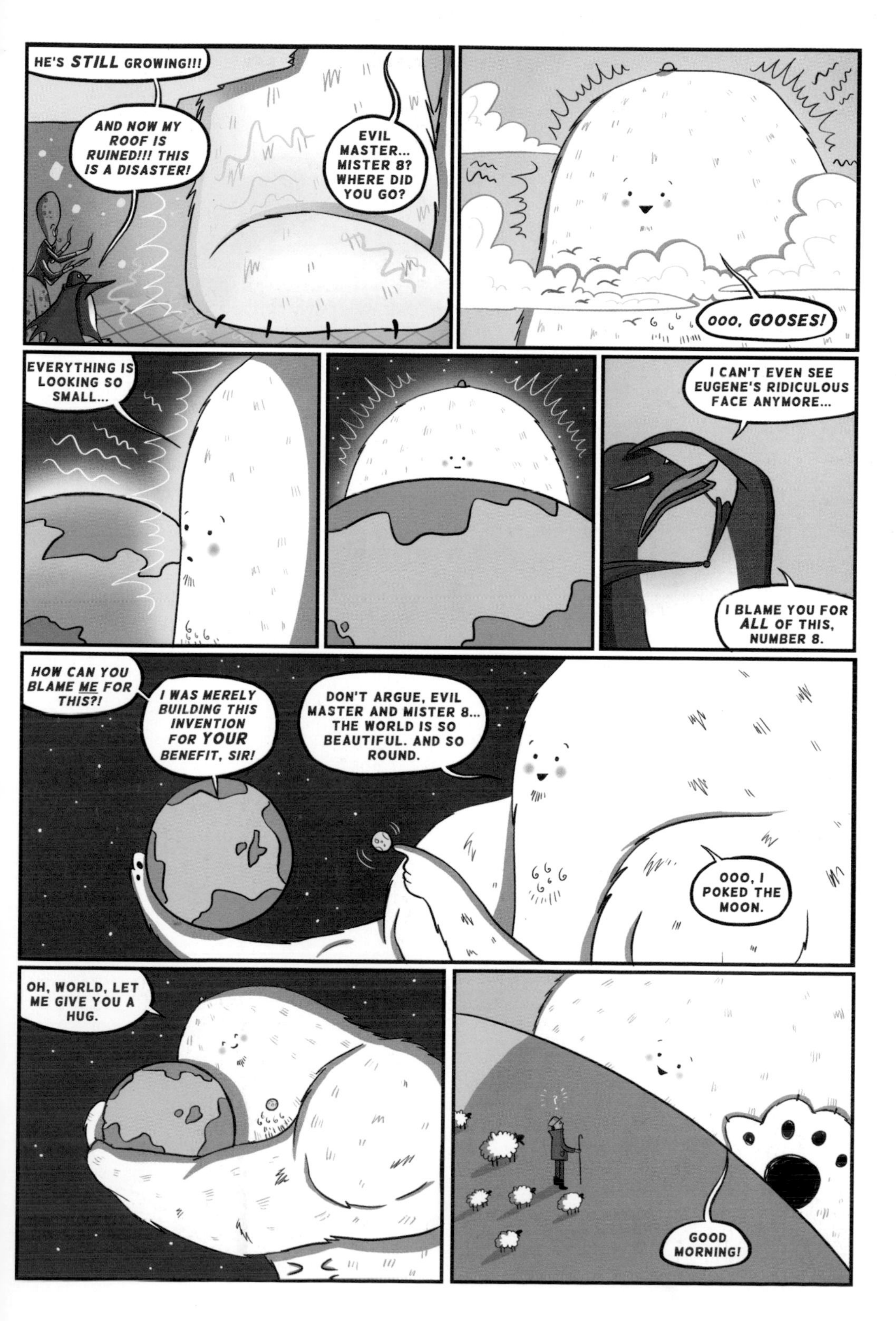
HE'S STILL GROWING!!!
AND NOW MY ROOF IS RUINED!!! THIS IS A DISASTER!
EVIL MASTER... MISTER 8? WHERE DID YOU GO?
OOO, GOOSES!
EVERYTHING IS LOOKING SO SMALL...
I CAN'T EVEN SEE EUGENE'S RIDICULOUS FACE ANYMORE...
I BLAME YOU FOR ALL OF THIS, NUMBER 8.
HOW CAN YOU BLAME ME FOR THIS?!
I WAS MERELY BUILDING THIS INVENTION FOR YOUR BENEFIT, SIR!
DON'T ARGUE, EVIL MASTER AND MISTER 8... THE WORLD IS SO BEAUTIFUL. AND SO ROUND.
OOO, I POKED THE MOON.
OH, WORLD, LET ME GIVE YOU A HUG.
GOOD MORNING!

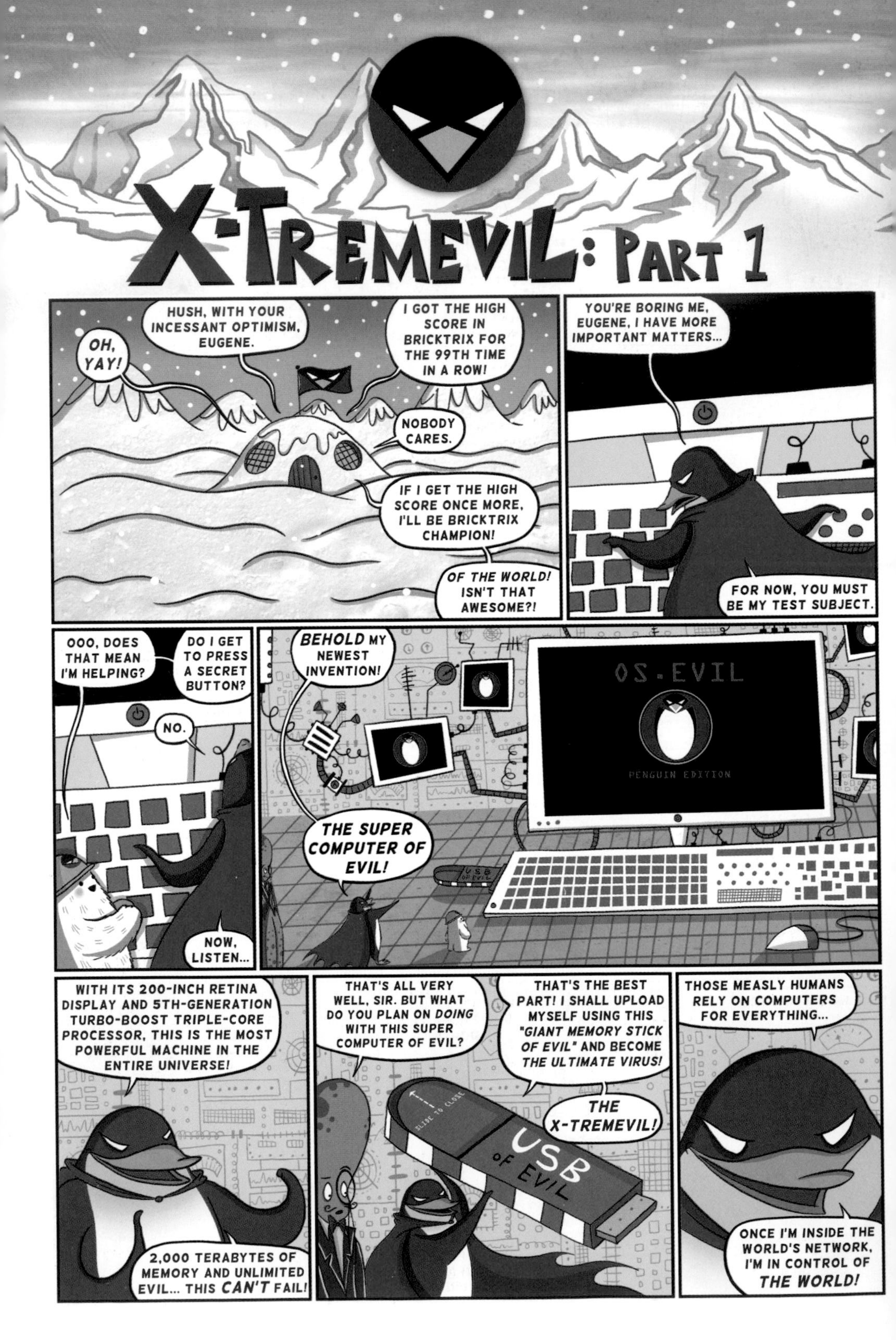

X-TREMEVIL: PART 1
OH, YAY!
HUSH, WITH YOUR INCESSANT OPTIMISM, EUGENE.
I GOT THE HIGH SCORE IN BRICKTRIX FOR THE 99TH TIME IN A ROW!
NOBODY CARES.
IF I GET THE HIGH SCORE ONCE MORE, I'LL BE BRICKTRIX CHAMPION!
OF THE WORLD! ISN'T THAT AWESOME?!
YOU'RE BORING ME, EUGENE, I HAVE MORE IMPORTANT MATTERS...
FOR NOW, YOU MUST BE MY TEST SUBJECT.
OOO, DOES THAT MEAN I'M HELPING?
DO I GET TO PRESS A SECRET BUTTON?
NO.
NOW, LISTEN...
BEHOLD MY NEWEST INVENTION!
OS-EVIL
PENGUIN EDITION
USB OF EVIL
THE SUPER COMPUTER OF EVIL!
WITH ITS 200-INCH RETINA DISPLAY AND 5TH-GENERATION TURBO-BOOST TRIPLE-CORE PROCESSOR, THIS IS THE MOST POWERFUL MACHINE IN THE ENTIRE UNIVERSE!
2,000 TERABYTES OF MEMORY AND UNLIMITED EVIL... THIS CAN'T FAIL!
THAT'S ALL VERY WELL, SIR. BUT WHAT DO YOU PLAN ON DOING WITH THIS SUPER COMPUTER OF EVIL?
THAT'S THE BEST PART! I SHALL UPLOAD MYSELF USING THIS "GIANT MEMORY STICK OF EVIL" AND BECOME THE ULTIMATE VIRUS!
THE X-TREMEVIL!
SLIDE TO CLOSE
USB OF EVIL
THOSE MEASLY HUMANS RELY ON COMPUTERS FOR EVERYTHING...
ONCE I'M INSIDE THE WORLD'S NETWORK, I'M IN CONTROL OF THE WORLD!

EUGENE. GO MAKE YOURSELF COMFY IN THE "GIANT MEMORY STICK OF EVIL"...
USB of EVIL
AND FOR THE LOVE OF EVIL, DON'T SING WHEN YOU'RE BEING UPLOADED.
WILL YOU TUCK ME IN, EVIL MASTER?
YOU'RE NOT GOING TO BED, EUGENE.
THERE'S A CHANCE YOUR UPLOAD WILL FAIL...
AND YOU'LL END UP FLOATING AROUND THE ETHERNET IN A TRILLION TINY PIECES.
"GIANT MEMORY STICK OF EVIL" ACTIVATED...
USB of EVIL
DETECTED...
BEGINNING UPLOAD...
UPLOAD PROGRESS 51%
ARE YOU SURE THIS IS GOING TO WORK, SIR?
OF COURSE NOT. THAT'S WHY I'M TESTING IT ON EUGENE FIRST.
UPLOAD COMPLETE
WHERE IS HE?
PATIENCE, SQUIDINGTON.
I SEE YOU, EVIL MASTER!
I FEEL OBLONG-Y.
I'M SO HAPPY!
PARP
I CAN'T BELIEVE YOU JUST DID THAT INSIDE MY SUPER COMPUTER OF EVIL...
WEEEEEEEE!
OKAY, EUGENE, I'M DOWNLOADING YOU BACK ONTO THE "GIANT MEMORY STICK OF EVIL"!
ARE ALL OF YOUR LIMBS STILL INTACT, EUGENE?
I THINK SO!
THEN MY PLAN IS READY FOR ACTION!
ONE HOUR LATER...
I'M READY FOR MY UPLOAD!
WORLD DOMINATION IS CALLING!
SLIDE TO CLOSE
HE'S UPLOADING... BOY, I HOPE THIS WORKS.
I DON'T THINK HIS EVIL SOUL COULD COPE WITH ANOTHER FAILURE...
X-TREMEVIL IS ONLINE!

EACH DOOR LEADS TO A DIFFERENT COMPUTER.
SO I CAN ACCESS ANY PROGRAM ON ANY COMPUTER ANYWHERE!
FIRST STOP, THE PRESIDENT OF THE USA! I FEEL HE NEEDS A FEW MORE PUPPIES ON HIS DESKTOP BACKGROUND.
COMPUTER OWNER: EVIL CAT
ONLINE
OR MAYBE I COULD DROP BY HERE FIRST.
footbook EVIL CAT Home Profile Friends
TIME FOR A BIT OF FUN BEFORE I TAKE OVER THE WORLD!
Update Status
THE BEST CAT IN THE WORLD AND EVEN BETTER LOOKING
EUGENE REJECTED YOUR FRIEND REQUEST
TODAY I'M THINKING OF BUYING A RADISH TO THROW AT YOU
YOU ADDED EUGENE AS A FRIEND
SOMEONE WAVED AT ME TODAY SO I TOOK THEIR CAR
Information
MUSTACHE CONNOISSEUR FUTURE WORLD LEADER
FUN FACTS: I WILL DEFEAT EVIL EMPEROR PENGUIN
footbook EVIL CAT Home Profile Friends
MY WORK HERE IS DONE. FOR NOW.
Update Status
I AM A BIG HAIRY PLATYPUS WHO EATS BUTTS FOR BREAKFAST
YOU ADDED EUGENE AS A FRIEND
SOMEONE WAVED AT ME TODAY SO I TOOK THEIR CAR
Information
THE STUPIDIST CAT EVER
FUN FACTS: I LOVE EMPEROR PENGUIN FOREVER
THAT WAS FUN... NOW BACK TO WORLD DOMINATION!
OOO, I SEE PAINT-PRO! I LOVE PAINT-PRO!
PAINT-PRO
File Edit View Image Options Help
I AM UNSTOPPABLE!
The world is MINE
EEP
PIXEL PERFECT!
OCTOMAIL NUMBER 8
COMPOSE
Inbox (12)
Evil Mail
Sent Mail
Drafts
Secret
Evil Empero
Evil Empero
Evil Empero
Julie
Eugene
Julie
Eugene
Eugene
BORING.
BORING.
EWW.
OOO!
NUMBER 8... YOU HAVE A SECRET ADMIRER!
JULIE HAS SENT YOU A WINK ON "TENTACLE TALK"...
SIR, I'M SURE HACKING INTO MY COMPUTER IS FUN FOR YOU, BUT YOU'RE MEANT TO BE TAKING OVER THE WORLD.
I'M EVIL EMPEROR PENGUIN. I CAN DO WHAT I LIKE.
THIS LOOKS INTERESTING. IT SAYS YOU'VE WON A LARGE SUM OF MONEY!
IT'S FROM THE KING OF SPAMLAND!
I CAN'T BELIEVE YOU HAVEN'T OPENED IT YET...
NO! DON'T OPEN THAT, SIR!
HOW RUDE.
OH, HUSH, JUST BECAUSE YOU WANT THE LARGE SUM OF MONEY ALL FOR YOURSELF!
SELFISH SQUID!
ERR, NUMBER 8. YOUR EMAIL IS MAKING LIGHTNING.
I AM RELEASED!
I AM TROJAN THE HUNK VIRUS.
I WILL DESTROY YOU AND ALL OF YOUR FILES.

X-TREMEVIL: PART 2
PREVIOUSLY ON EEP...
THIS GUY...
OPENED THIS...
AND UNLEASHED THIS GUY.
YOU CLEARLY HAVE NO IDEA WHO I AM...
I AM THE ONE AND ONLY EVIL EMPEROR PENGUIN AND-
WHOA... SOMEONE WORKS OUT. YOU'RE HARDER THAN A ROCK!
I SHALL DELETE YOU ONE LIMB AT A TIME.
YOU'RE NOT HERE FOR CHITCHAT ARE YOU...
YOU KNOW NOT WHAT I AM CAPABLE OF, SMALL FEEBLE PIXEL.
INK
HEY! YOU DID NOT JUST ERASE MY CAPE WITH THAT WAND OF YOURS...
YOINK!
GOT YOUR LOINCLOTH!
Exit
SWOOP!
SWOOOOOOSH!
-GASP-
YOU ERASE MY CAPE-I TAKE YOUR SKIRT! SIMPLE!
I NEED TO LOSE THAT PUNK... I'LL HIDE IN HERE!
ONLINE
ONLINE
WHO KNOWS WHERE THIS LEADS...
WHOA!
HEY! WHY ARE YOU IN SUCH A RUSH?
YOU'D MAKE A GOOD CAPE Y'KNOW...
RUN, DUDE!
WHAT IS THIS PLACE?!
GOOD GRIEF! CLOSE YOUR MOUTH THIS INSTANT! DO YOU HAVE NO MANNERS?!
DO NOT COME ANY CLOSER YOU ROUND... PIE THING!

WHY DOESN'T ANYBODY LISTEN AROUND HERE?!
OH BOY...
YOU ARE MINE!
THAT NEW SKIRT LOOKS JUST LOVELY...
IT'S YOUR CAPE...
DUDE! GRAB THAT SHINY BALL THINGY!
INVINCI-BALL ACTIVATED
HUZZAH!
IT WORKED!
YEAH THAT'S RIGHT... RUN! YOU BIG LOIN-CLOTH!
ONLINE
SEARCH ENGINE ROOM
YOU CAN'T RUN FROM ME! I'M AN INVINCIBLE CIRCLE NOW!
OH... THAT WORE OFF.
SHPPP!
Smoogle search
YOU WILL PAY!
Smoogle search
HOW TO DELETE A HUNKY VIRUS
QUICK! SEARCH! ANSWERS NOW!
Smoogle Search not responding
OK
YOU HAVE GOT TO BE KIDDING.
YOU KNOW YOU'RE OUT OF OPTIONS WHEN YOUR LAST RESORT IS A BIN.
TROJAN WILL DELETE YOU!
YOU CAN NOT HIDE!
I CAN DETECT YOUR PRESENCE IN THE RECYCLING BIN.
GREAT.
31
I HAVE YOU NOW!
Open
Explore
Empty Recycle Bin
Create Shortcut
Properties
CRRRRRNCH
ERGH... WHERE AM I NOW?
I CAN HEAR AN ANNOYINGLY CATCHY TUNE.

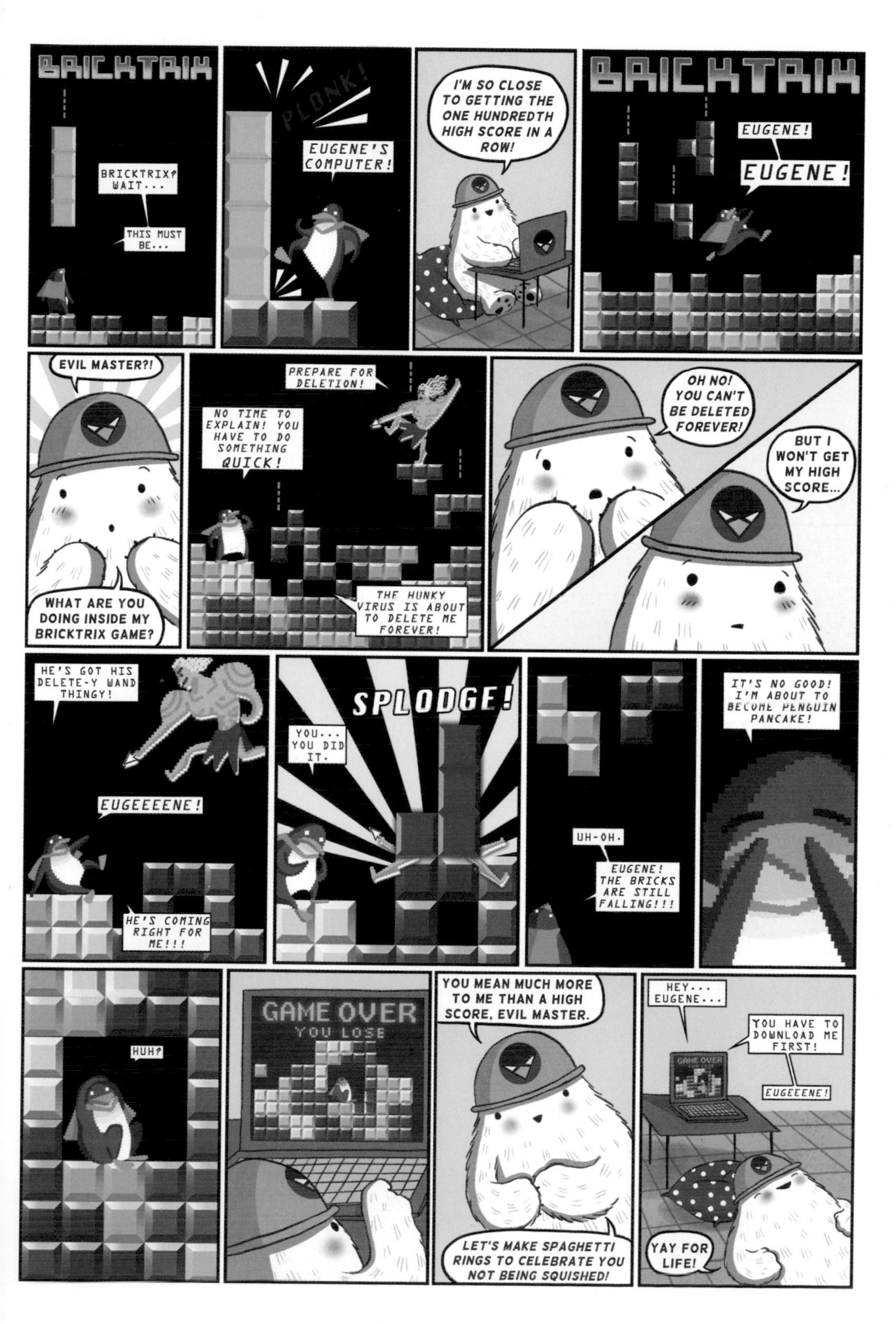
BRICKTRIX
BRICKTRIX? WAIT...
THIS MUST BE...
PLONK!
EUGENE'S COMPUTER!
I'M SO CLOSE TO GETTING THE ONE HUNDREDTH HIGH SCORE IN A ROW!
BRICKTRIX
EUGENE!
EUGENE!
EVIL MASTER?!
WHAT ARE YOU DOING INSIDE MY BRICKTRIX GAME?
PREPARE FOR DELETION!
NO TIME TO EXPLAIN! YOU HAVE TO DO SOMETHING QUICK!
THE HUNKY VIRUS IS ABOUT TO DELETE ME FOREVER!
OH NO! YOU CAN'T BE DELETED FOREVER!
BUT I WON'T GET MY HIGH SCORE...
HE'S GOT HIS DELETE-Y WAND THINGY!
EUGEEEENE!
HE'S COMING RIGHT FOR ME!!!
SPLODGE!
YOU... YOU DID IT.
UH-OH.
EUGENE! THE BRICKS ARE STILL FALLING!!!
IT'S NO GOOD! I'M ABOUT TO BECOME PENGUIN PANCAKE!
HUH?
GAME OVER
YOU LOSE
YOU MEAN MUCH MORE TO ME THAN A HIGH SCORE, EVIL MASTER.
LET'S MAKE SPAGHETTI RINGS TO CELEBRATE YOU NOT BEING SQUISHED!
HEY... EUGENE...
YOU HAVE TO DOWNLOAD ME FIRST!
EUGEEENE!
YAY FOR LIFE!

PIGEON-HOLED

I NEED YOU TO DISPOSE OF THE PIGEON OUTSIDE.
PIGEON?
BUT WE DON'T GET PIGEONS AROUND HERE, SIR...
EVIL PLANZ
DO NOT QUESTION ME, SQUID-FACE!
REMOVE SAID PIGEON, NOW!
BEDROOM OF EVIL
EVIL PLANZ
OKAY, WHERE WAS I...?
OH YES, PLOTTING THE FALL OF THE HUMAN RACE...
DONK!
EVIL
HUH?
YOU!
NUMBER 8!!! GET HERE RIGHT NOW!
YOU CALLED, SIR?
I TOLD YOU TO REMOVE THAT PIGEON! GET IT OUT OF HERE!
SIR, I CAN'T SEE A PIGEON ANYWHERE.
IT WAS RIGHT THERE!
MAYBE YOU SHOULD TAKE A DAY OFF, SIR...
I'LL GIVE YOUR FACE A DAY OFF IN A MINUTE!
NOW, GO FIND THAT STUPID PIGEON!!!

ERGH, I CAN'T BELIEVE I'VE HAD TO WORK IN THE KITCHEN OF EVIL!
AT LEAST THAT STUPID PIGEON IS GONE.
OKAY... THIS TIME I MEAN BUSINESS. PREPARE TO BECOME—
BONG!
A PIGEON PANCAKE!
GOOD.
NOW THAT'S TAKEN CARE OF, I CAN FINISH MY EVIL PLAN IN PEACE.
EVIL MASTER?
KNOCK KNOCK
I DIDN'T EXPECT TO FIND YOU IN HERE...
THAT'S BECAUSE THIS PIGEON KEEPS DISTRACTING ME!
SQUID-FACE NUMBER 8 SEEMS INCAPABALE OF GETTING RID OF THE THING!
I DON'T SEE A PIGEON, EVIL MASTER.
BUT I WOULD LOVE ONE AS A PET!
ONE HOUR LATER...
I GUARANTEE YOU, THAT PIGEON WILL TURN UP ANY MINUTE NOW...
AND WHEN IT DOES, I'LL TURN IT INTO DUST!
PERISCOPE OF EVIL
DUST?!

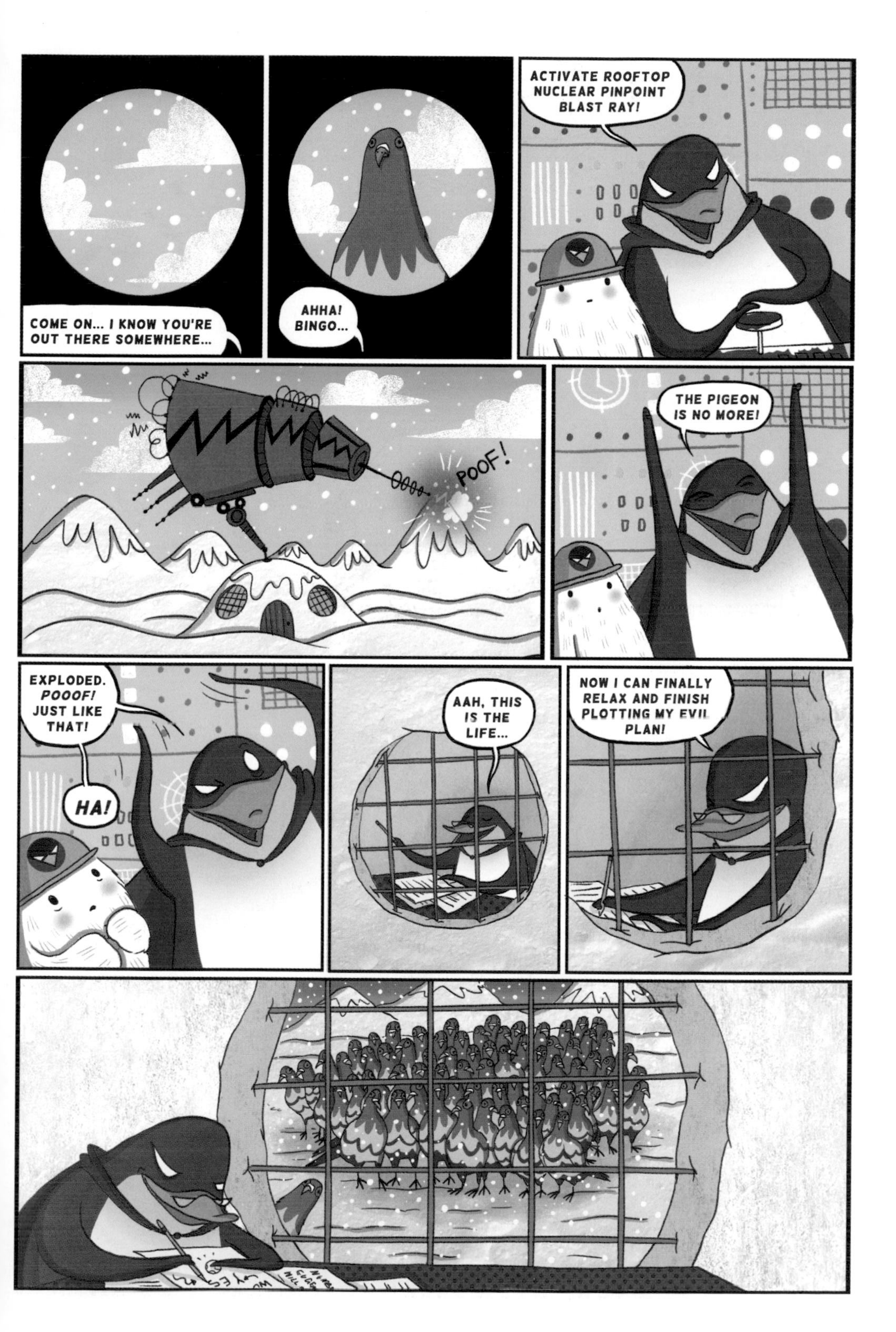
COME ON... I KNOW YOU'RE OUT THERE SOMEWHERE...
AHHA! BINGO...
ACTIVATE ROOFTOP NUCLEAR PINPOINT BLAST RAY!
POOF!
THE PIGEON IS NO MORE!
EXPLODED. POOOF! JUST LIKE THAT!
HA!
AAH, THIS IS THE LIFE...
NOW I CAN FINALLY RELAX AND FINISH PLOTTING MY EVIL PLAN!

POP GOES THE EASEL
EUGENE, WHY ARE YOU MULTICOLORED?
I'VE BEEN PAINTING, EVIL MASTER. I'M GOING TO HAVE AN ART EXHIBITION...
I'VE CALLED IT... *HAPPY FACES.*
LOOK, THIS ONE IS BASED ON YOU, EVIL MASTER!
HAPPY
HMMM...
I'VE HAD A GENIUS IDEA, EUGENE...
OF COURSE, I *AM* A GENIUS!
BUT ANYWAY...
THOSE HUMANS LOVE A GOOD PIECE OF ART...
HAPPY
ESPECIALLY THOSE SNOOTY WORLD-LEADER TYPES.
IF THEY WERE INVITED TO A PRIVATE VIEW OF *THE BEST ART EXHIBITION IN THE WORLD*, THEY'D JUMP AT THE CHANCE!
ONCE ALL THE WORLD LEADERS ARE UNDER ONE ROOF, I CAN ZAP THEM WITH MY "PAINT PALETTE OF EVIL"!
IT'LL TRANSFORM ANYTHING INTO A TWO-DIMENSIONAL IMAGE!
TRIGGER BUTTON LOOKS LIKE PAINT!
ME
ZZZZAP!
WORLD LEADER
TURNED INTO A PAINTING!
ALL OF THE WORLD LEADERS WILL BE TURNED INTO PAINTINGS AND THEN I SHALL TAKE OVER THE **WORLD!!!**
I'LL EVEN MAKE SURE THEY HAVE A PRETTY FRAME AROUND THEM, SO YOU CAN'T SAY I DON'T CARE, *EH!*

THE BAIT GALLERY
THE BEST ART EXHIBITION IN THE WORLD HOSTED BY VAN-EEP
ENTRANCE
WAIT HERE
WHEN I RECEIVED MY PERSONAL INVITATION TO A PRIVATE VIEW HOSTED BY VAN-EEP, HOW COULD I SAY NO?!
DEFINITELY WORTH TRAVELING TO ANTARCTICA FOR!
HAVE YOU HEARD OF VAN-EEP BEFORE?
I LIKED VAN-EEP BEFORE HE WAS COOL...
I'M GOING TO ANALYZE SO MUCH ART TODAY...
I'VE NEVER SEEN SO MANY WORLD LEADERS IN ONE PLACE!
FOOLS!
I MANAGED TO STEAL EVERY FAMOUS PAINTING YOU CAN THINK OF...
EVEN THE MOANING LISA...
RIGHT, I JUST NEED TO GIVE THE "PAINT PALETTE OF EVIL" A TEST RUN ON THIS STUPID TOY.
BUT, EVIL MASTER! THAT'S MY VERY SPECIAL UNICORN TOY!
STAY BACK, EUGENE...
ACTIVATING "PAINT PALETTE OF EVIL"...
NO, EUGENE!
OH, GEEZ.
EVIL MASTER...?
I FEEL... FLAT.
EUGENE! I TOLD YOU TO STAY BACK, YOU BIG PARSNIP!!!
BUT YOU WERE GOING TO ZAP MY SPECIAL UNICORN TOY.

ARGH! I'LL HAVE TO FIGURE OUT HOW TO REWIRE THE "PAINT PALETTE OF EVIL" SO THAT IT TURNS 2-D BACK TO 3-D...
OKAY, THIS SHOULD DO IT...
I NEED TO PEE.
LOOK AT MY ABSTRACT ABILITIES, EVIL MASTER!
OKAY, THAT DEFINITELY DIDN'T WORK...
RIGHT, I'VE SWAPPED THE BLUE AND RED WIRE, IT SHOULD WORK THIS TIME!
WHYYYYY WON'T HE STOP SCREEEEAMIIIIING?!
LET'S JUST GET RID OF THIS WIRE...
PHEW, HE WAS LOUD... OOO, AN APPLE.
ON MY FACE.
NOPE.
COME ON!
OH, HEY THERE, NICE LADY. WHY DO YOUR EYES KEEP FOLLOWING ME?
AGAIN!
POINTING...
ZZZAP!
ARRRRGH! WHY WON'T IT WORK?!
DON'T BE ANGRY, EVIL MASTER. I'M DOING FINE...
OH, DEAR... IT WON'T STOP ZAPPING...

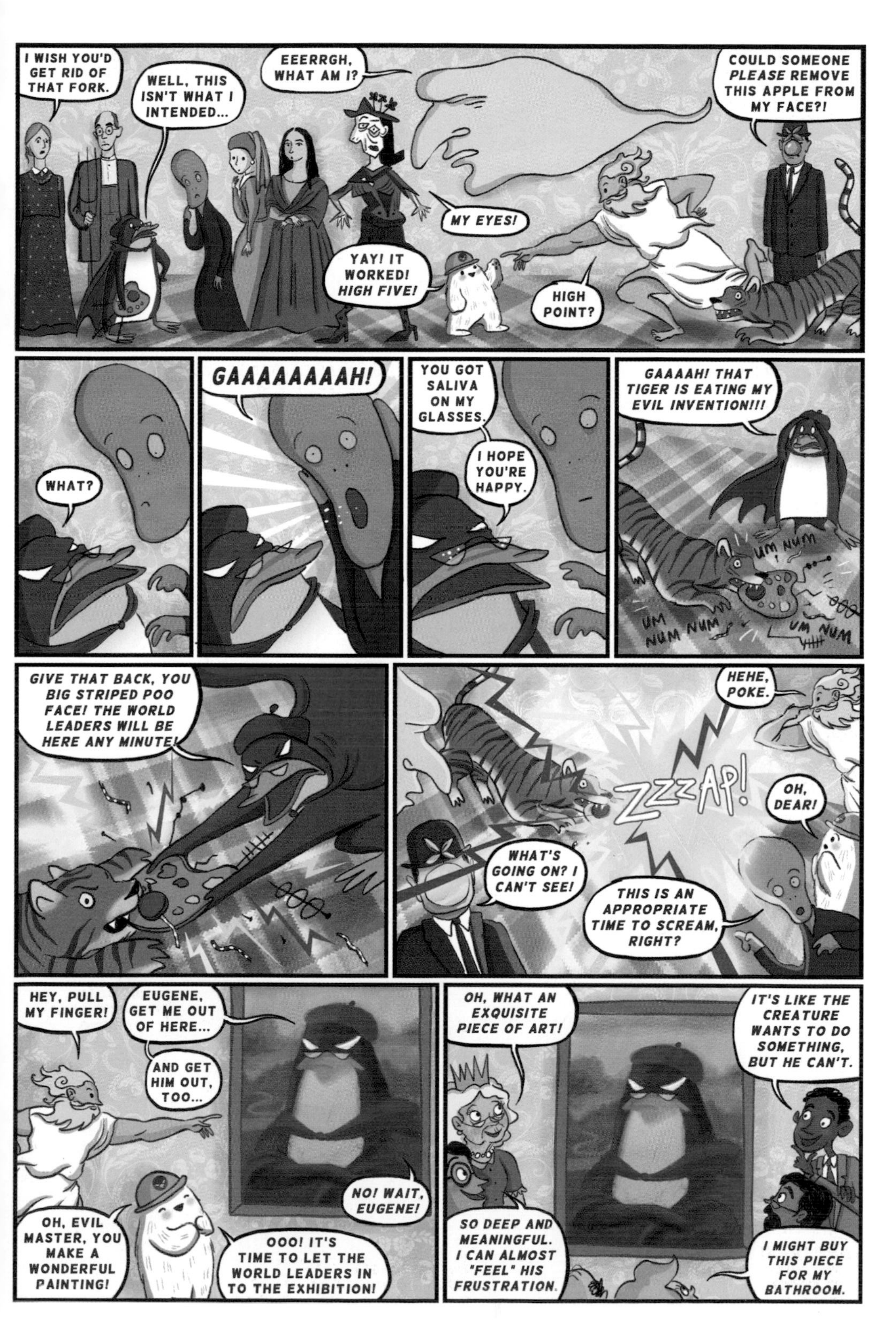
I WISH YOU'D GET RID OF THAT FORK.
WELL, THIS ISN'T WHAT I INTENDED...
EEERRGH, WHAT AM I?
COULD SOMEONE PLEASE REMOVE THIS APPLE FROM MY FACE?!
MY EYES!
YAY! IT WORKED! HIGH FIVE!
HIGH POINT?
WHAT?
GAAAAAAAAH!
YOU GOT SALIVA ON MY GLASSES.
I HOPE YOU'RE HAPPY.
GAAAAH! THAT TIGER IS EATING MY EVIL INVENTION!!!
UM NUM
UM NUM NUM
UM NUM
GIVE THAT BACK, YOU BIG STRIPED POO FACE! THE WORLD LEADERS WILL BE HERE ANY MINUTE!
HEHE, POKE.
ZZZAP!
OH, DEAR!
WHAT'S GOING ON? I CAN'T SEE!
THIS IS AN APPROPRIATE TIME TO SCREAM, RIGHT?
HEY, PULL MY FINGER!
EUGENE, GET ME OUT OF HERE...
AND GET HIM OUT, TOO...
NO! WAIT, EUGENE!
OH, EVIL MASTER, YOU MAKE A WONDERFUL PAINTING!
OOO! IT'S TIME TO LET THE WORLD LEADERS IN TO THE EXHIBITION!
OH, WHAT AN EXQUISITE PIECE OF ART!
IT'S LIKE THE CREATURE WANTS TO DO SOMETHING, BUT HE CAN'T.
SO DEEP AND MEANINGFUL. I CAN ALMOST "FEEL" HIS FRUSTRATION.
I MIGHT BUY THIS PIECE FOR MY BATHROOM.

WHAT'S NEW, PUSSY CAT?
OOO, LOOK. ANOTHER BOLT OF LIGHTNING! DID YOU SEE THAT, EVIL MASTER?
EVIL MASTER?
I THINK HE'S HIDING UNDER SOME BLANKETS IN THE BEDROOM OF EVIL.
OH, OKAY, MISTER 8.
OH, I DO LOVE THUNDER-STORMS.
I WISH WE HAD THEM MORE OFTEN IN ANTARCTICA!
OH, DEAR, SOMEONE'S LEFT A BOX OUTSIDE!
GASP
OH, MY! THERE'S A POOR LITTLE KITTY CAT INSIDE!
I HAVE TO GO SAVE IT!
WHO COULD LEAVE YOU OUTSIDE LIKE THIS?!
LET'S GET YOU SAFE INSIDE.

YOU CAN STAY HERE. I'M SURE EVIL MASTER AND MISTER 8 WON'T MIND.
ALTHOUGH, LAST TIME WE ADOPTED A CAT, HE TURNED OUT TO BE OUR ARCHNEMESIS.
BUT WHAT ARE THE CHANCES OF THAT HAPPENING AGAIN?! HEHE!
LET'S TAKE YOU FOR A WALK AROUND THE EVIL LAIR.
THIS IS THE CORRIDOR OF EVIL...
AND BEHIND THAT TOP-SECRET DOOR IS WHERE WE KEEP ALL OF EVIL MASTER'S SPAGHETTI RINGS!
LET ME INTRODUCE YOU TO EVIL MASTER...
OF EVI
KNOCK KNOCK
EVIL MASTER?
ARE YOU SCARED OF THE THUNDERSTORM, EVIL MASTER?
NO!
I'M JUST CHECKING THE UNDERSIDE OF MY BLANKET. DO YOU HAVE A PROBLEM WITH THAT?!
WELL, THAT'S OKAY, THEN!
I'D LIKE YOU TO MEET MY NEW PET!
SHE DOESN'T HAVE A NAME YET...
BUT I THINK I'LL CALL HER DEBRA.
?
DEBRA?
YEAH, DEBRA WORKS.

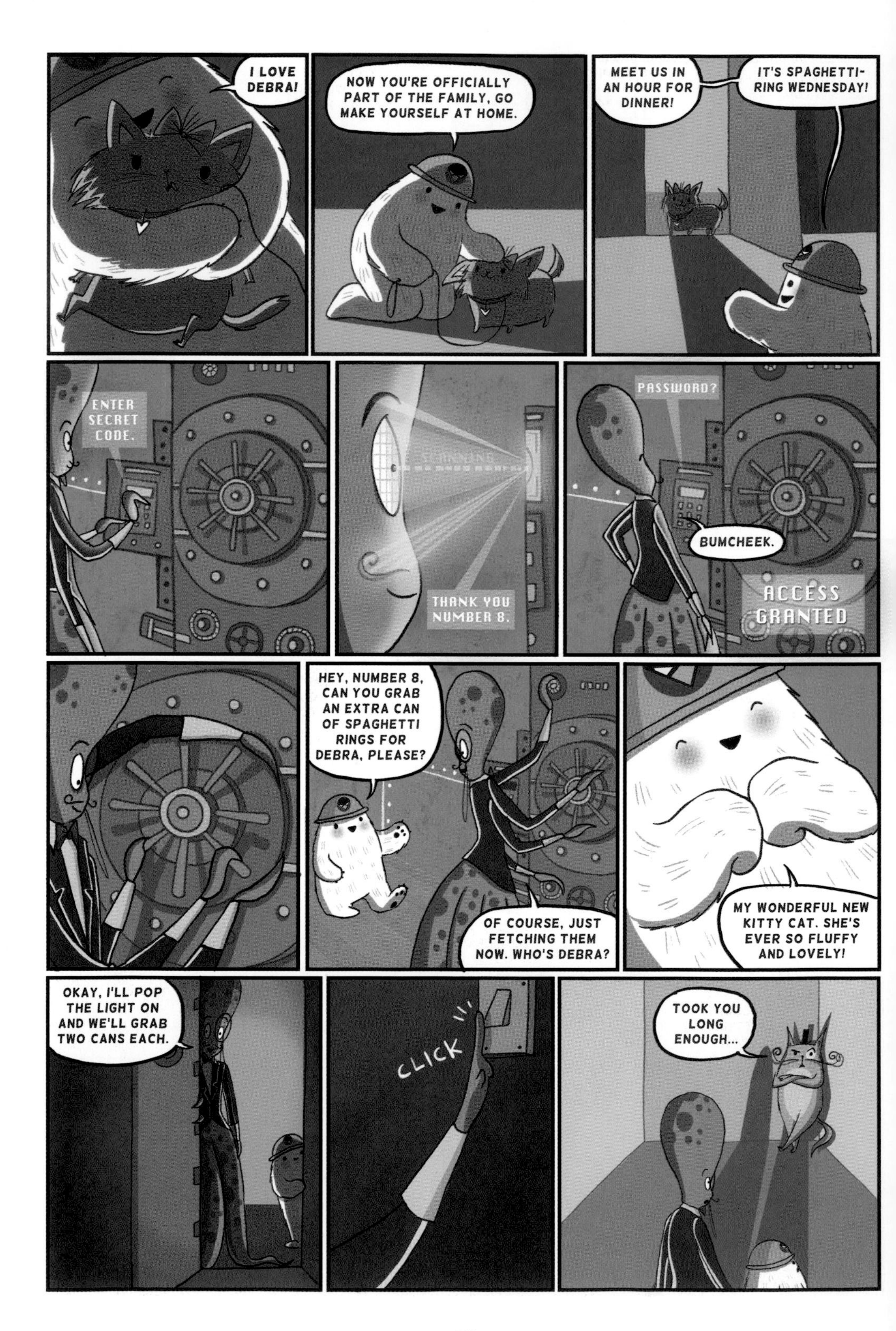
I LOVE DEBRA!
NOW YOU'RE OFFICIALLY PART OF THE FAMILY, GO MAKE YOURSELF AT HOME.
MEET US IN AN HOUR FOR DINNER!
IT'S SPAGHETTI-RING WEDNESDAY!
ENTER SECRET CODE.
SCANNING
THANK YOU NUMBER 8.
PASSWORD?
BUMCHEEK.
ACCESS GRANTED
HEY, NUMBER 8, CAN YOU GRAB AN EXTRA CAN OF SPAGHETTI RINGS FOR DEBRA, PLEASE?
OF COURSE, JUST FETCHING THEM NOW. WHO'S DEBRA?
MY WONDERFUL NEW KITTY CAT. SHE'S EVER SO FLUFFY AND LOVELY!
OKAY, I'LL POP THE LIGHT ON AND WE'LL GRAB TWO CANS EACH.
CLICK
TOOK YOU LONG ENOUGH...

EVIL CAT!!! HOW DID YOU GET IN HERE?!
AND WHAT HAVE YOU DONE WITH ALL THE SPAGHETTI RINGS?!
I DON'T KNOW, AND I HAVEN'T TOUCHED THEM...
MAYBE YOU SHOULD ASK YOUR LITTLE FRIEND DEBRA.
YOU LEAVE DEBRA OUT OF THIS, YOU BIG FAT CAT!
HEY NOW, I LOST TWO POUNDS LAST WEEK.
WELL, WHAT ARE WE MEANT TO THINK? WE FIND YOU IN THE TOP-SECRET SPAGHETTI-RING STORAGE ROOM, AND THE SPAGHETTI RINGS ARE MISSING...
DON'T YOU THINK I HAVE ENOUGH SPAGHETTI RINGS THANKS TO THE LIFETIME SUBSCRIPTION YOU SO KINDLY TRICKED ME INTO?!
THEN WHAT ARE YOU DOING IN HERE?!
I DON'T REALLY KNOW... LAST THING I REMEMBER, I WAS SEARCHING ONLINE FOR A NEW SHOWER CAP.
NEXT THING I KNOW, I'M IN HERE BEING BLAMED FOR SOMETHING I DIDN'T DO!
AND HOW DO YOU KNOW ABOUT DEBRA? YOU'VE NEVER EVEN MET HER...
PAH! KNOW ABOUT HER?! SHE'S MY THIRTEENTH COUSIN TWICE REMOVED.
HER REAL NAME IS EVELYN. THOUGH, SHE PREFERS TO SPELL IT, *EVILYN.*
AND IF YOU THINK I'M BAD, SHE'S PROBABLY THIRTEEN TIMES WORSE...
I CAN'T BELIEVE IT... I THOUGHT SHE WAS A LOVELY KITTY CAT.
THERE, THERE, EUGENE. HOW COULD YOU HAVE KNOWN.
OH, COME ON. SHE OOZES EVILNESS.
GLAD TO SEE YOU'RE ALL GETTING ALONG, 'CAUSE YOU'RE GONNA BE IN HERE FOR A REEEEALLY LONG TIME!
EEEEHEHEHEHEE!
SLAM
LOCK
CLICK
LOCK
CLICK
LOCK
YEP, THAT'S MY COUSIN, ALL RIGHT.

Rainbows to the Rescue

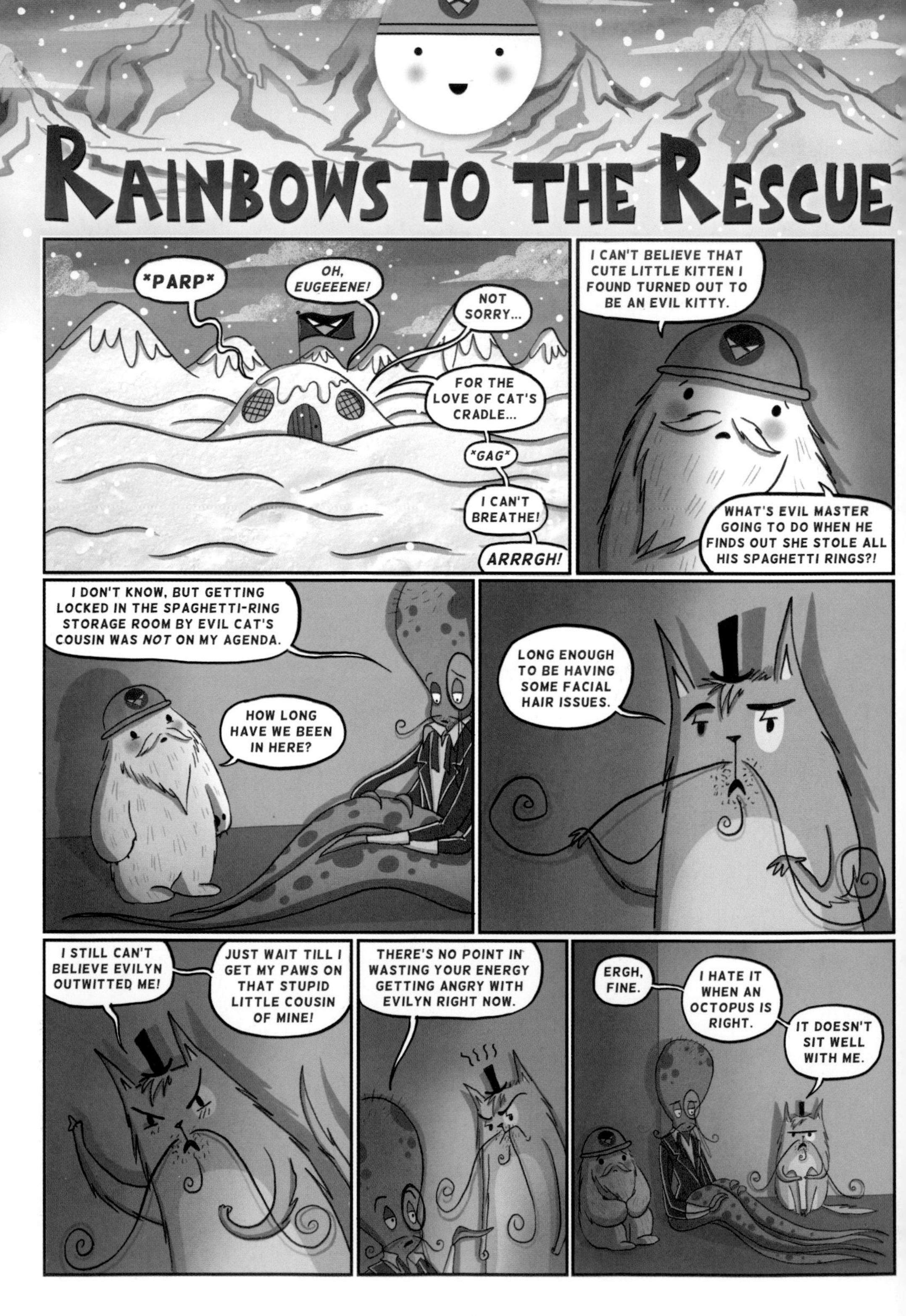

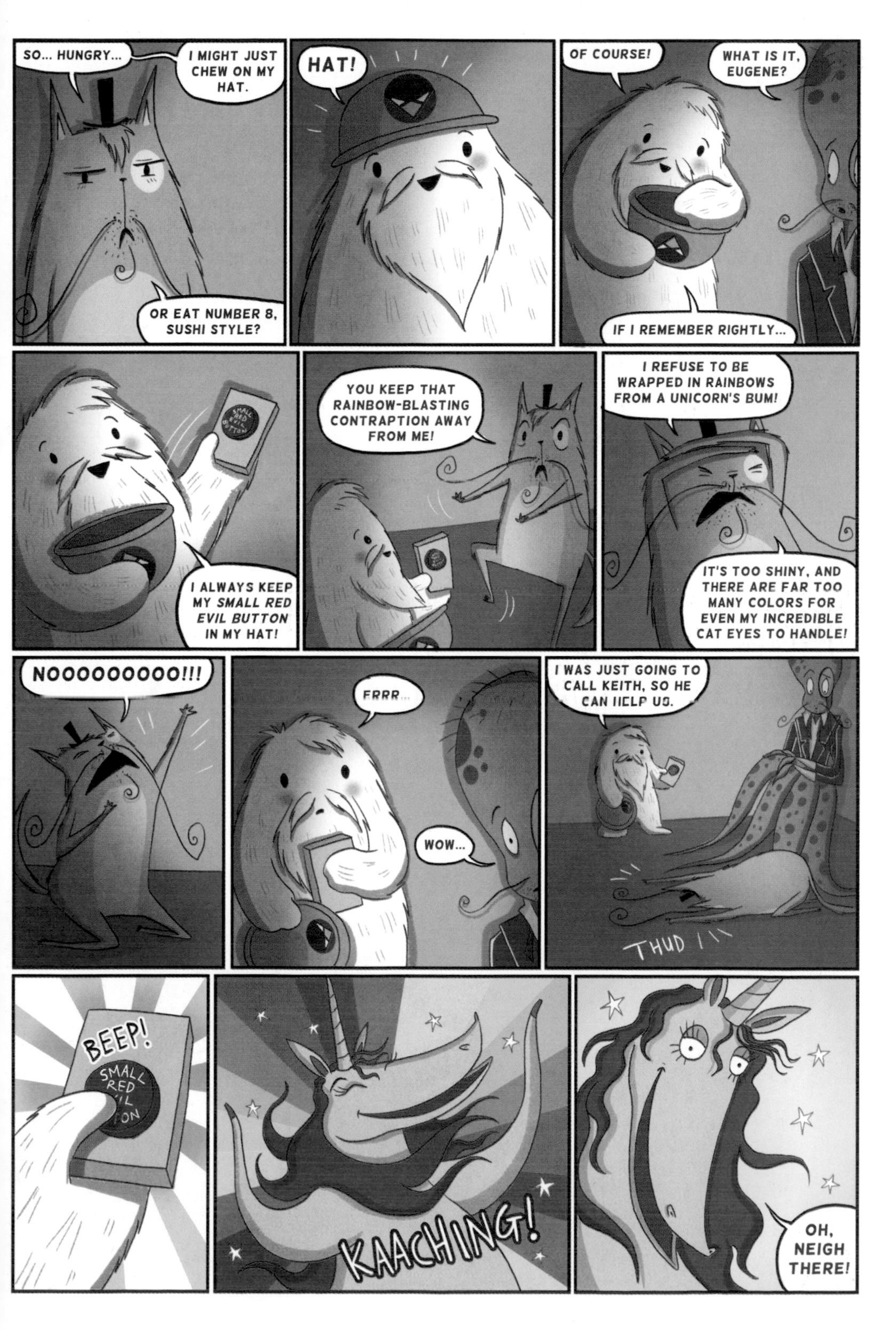
SO... HUNGRY...
I MIGHT JUST CHEW ON MY HAT.
OR EAT NUMBER 8, SUSHI STYLE?
HAT!
OF COURSE!
WHAT IS IT, EUGENE?
IF I REMEMBER RIGHTLY...
SMALL RED EVIL BUTTON
I ALWAYS KEEP MY *SMALL RED EVIL BUTTON* IN MY HAT!
YOU KEEP THAT RAINBOW-BLASTING CONTRAPTION AWAY FROM ME!
I REFUSE TO BE WRAPPED IN RAINBOWS FROM A UNICORN'S BUM!
IT'S TOO SHINY, AND THERE ARE FAR TOO MANY COLORS FOR EVEN MY INCREDIBLE CAT EYES TO HANDLE!
NOOOOOOOOO!!!
ERRR...
WOW...
I WAS JUST GOING TO CALL KEITH, SO HE CAN HELP US.
THUD
BEEP!
SMALL RED
KAACHING!
OH, NEIGH THERE!

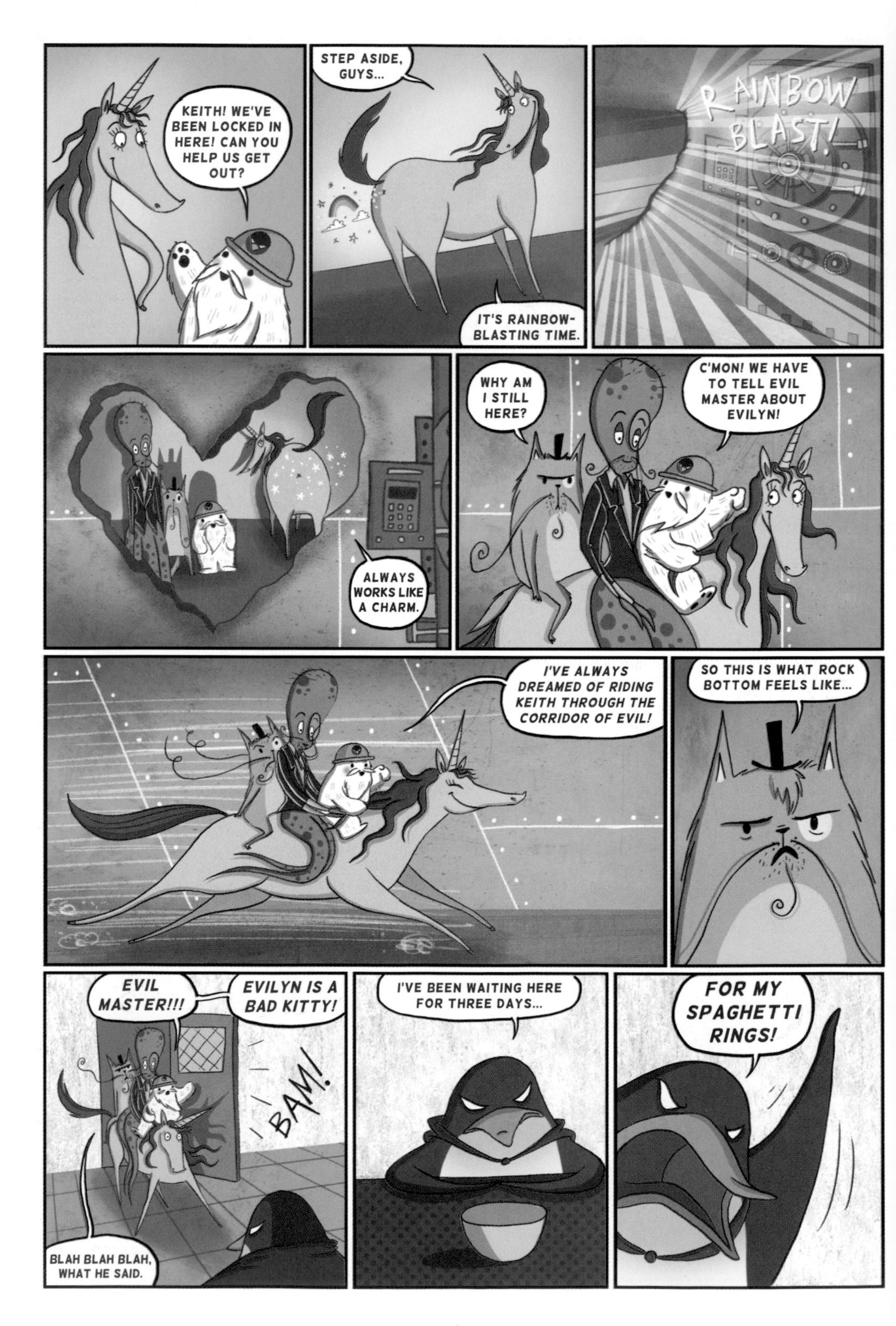
KEITH! WE'VE BEEN LOCKED IN HERE! CAN YOU HELP US GET OUT?
STEP ASIDE, GUYS...
IT'S RAINBOW-BLASTING TIME.
RAINBOW BLAST!
ALWAYS WORKS LIKE A CHARM.
WHY AM I STILL HERE?
C'MON! WE HAVE TO TELL EVIL MASTER ABOUT EVILYN!
I'VE ALWAYS DREAMED OF RIDING KEITH THROUGH THE CORRIDOR OF EVIL!
SO THIS IS WHAT ROCK BOTTOM FEELS LIKE...
EVIL MASTER!!!
EVILYN IS A BAD KITTY!
BAM!
BLAH BLAH BLAH, WHAT HE SAID.
I'VE BEEN WAITING HERE FOR THREE DAYS...
FOR MY SPAGHETTI RINGS!

NICE OF YOU TO SAY HELLO TO YOUR GUEST...
WHAT ARE YOU DOING HERE?!
I'M WELL, AND HOW ARE YOU?
AND WHY IS YOUR FACIAL HAIR ALL LONG AND CREEPY?!
DIDN'T YOUR MOTHER EVER TELL YOU NOT TO STAND ON TABLES?
HEY, YOU! HOW'S TRICKS?
ERGH, KEITH.
I'M JUST NEVER THAT ENTHUSED TO SEE YOU...
NOW, IT'S ALL VERY WELL HAVING THIS ODD ARCHNEMESIS/RAINBOW-LOVING UNICORN REUNION, BUT WHAT REALLY MATTERS RIGHT NOW IS...
WHERE MY SPAGHETTI RINGS ARE!!!
UM... THEY'VE BEEN STOLEN, EVIL MASTER.
BY EVILYN... SHE'S A REALLY BAD KITTY CAT.
WHAT?!
GOOD GRIEF, THEY'RE JUST SPAGHETTI RINGS, WHAT'S THE BIG DEAL?!
THEY DON'T EVEN TASTE GOOD...
WHAT...DID...YOU... JUST...SAY...?!
EUGENE, DO YOUR THING...
BEEP!
IT WOULD BE MY PLEASURE, EVIL MASTER!
NOT AGAIN!!!
AT LEAST THAT'S ONE PROBLEM OUT OF THE WAY...
AND DON'T YOU WORRY, WE'LL FIND YOUR SPAGHETTI RINGS, EVIL MASTER!
BUT WHAT AM I MEANT TO EAT NOW?!
OH, I HAVE JUST THE THING!
I THINK YOU'LL LOVE IT!
IT'S A UNICORN SPECIALITY.
RAINBOW SOUP... ARE YOU KIDDING ME?

THE ONE RING
BING BONG BING BONG CHRISTMAS!
LOOK! I'M A CHRISTMAS TREE!
STOP THAT, EUGENE!
YOU'RE PUTTING STRAIN ON MY BRAIN CELLS.
BUT, EVIL MASTER, IT'S CHRISTMAS TOMORROW! THE MERRIEST TIME OF THE YEAR. WHY AREN'T YOU BEING MERRY?
THE SPAGHETTI-RING STORAGE ROOM IS STILL EMPTY, EUGENE. CHRISTMAS ISN'T THE SAME WITHOUT THOSE RINGS.
NOW LEAVE ME BE. I MUST MOURN.
DEALING WITH RING LOSS
OH, OF COURSE, EVIL MASTER...
NOW I'M SAD.
I AM A SAD TREE.
I FEEL SO BAD FOR EVIL MASTER. HE LOVES SPAGHETTI RINGS SO MUCH...
WHAT IF WE NEVER FIND THEM EVER AGAIN?
HUH?
OOO, SHINY!
GASP
IT'S A SPAGHETTI RING...

YOU'RE OUR ONLY HOPE, LITTLE SPAGHETTI RING!
YOU'LL MAKE EVIL MASTER EVER SO HAPPY!
MY PRECIOUS!
HEY, EUGENE! WHAT'RE YOU DOING DOWN THERE?
OH, HELLO, GARY!
BLOOMIN' BOTTOMS, IS THAT WHAT I THINK IT IS?!
YOUR THOUGHTS ARE CORRECT, GARY!
IT'S A SPAGHETTI RING!
I FOUND IT ON THE FLOOR ALL ON ITS OWN.
EVIL MASTER IS GOING TO BE SO HAPPY WHEN I SHOW HIM!
I SHOULD GIVE IT TO EVIL MASTER. YOU'RE VERY BUSY BEING TOP MINION AND ALL...
BUT I FOUND IT... I SHOULD GIVE IT TO HIM, REALLY.
HEY, GUYS! WHAT'S GOING ON HERE?
HI, NEILL.
OH! IS THAT A SPAGHETTI RING?!
YES, AND EUGENE WON'T LET ME GIVE IT TO EVIL MASTER!
DON'T BE SILLY, CLEARLY I SHOULD GIVE IT TO HIM!
NO, NEILL, YOU'LL END UP LOSING IT. YOU'RE ALWAYS LOSING THINGS.
HELLO, FRIENDS!
OH NO, IT'S LORENZO.
NO WAY! A SPAGHETTI RING?!
WELL, ISN'T THIS EXCITING! IMAGINE HOW PLEASED EVIL MASTER WILL BE WHEN HE SEES THIS!
I SHOULD GIVE IT TO HIM! SAVE YOU ALL THE TROUBLE.
HEY!
OI!
I THINK I'M JUST GOING TO GO GIVE IT TO EVIL MASTER NOW...

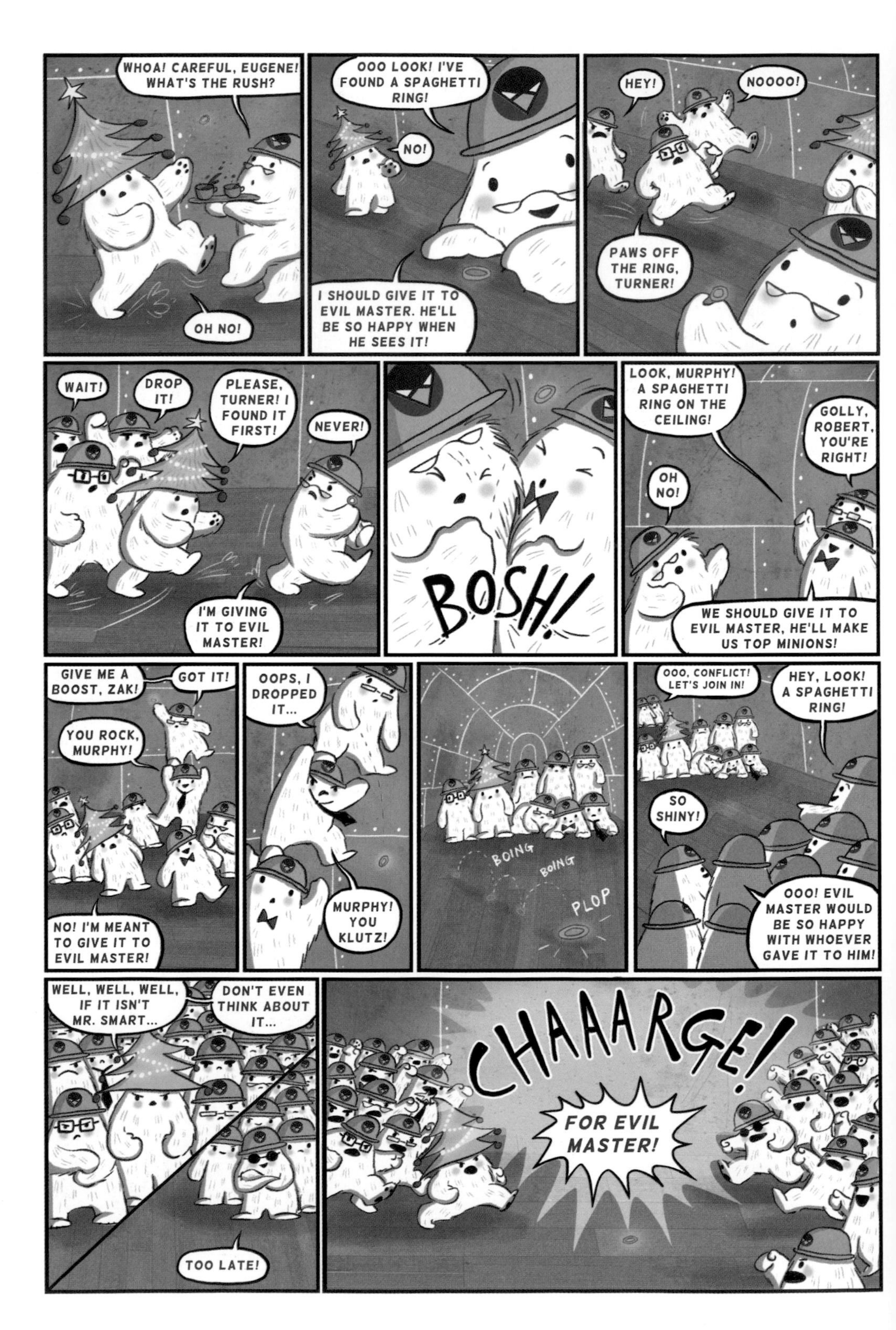
WHOA! CAREFUL, EUGENE! WHAT'S THE RUSH?
OH NO!
OOO LOOK! I'VE FOUND A SPAGHETTI RING!
NO!
I SHOULD GIVE IT TO EVIL MASTER. HE'LL BE SO HAPPY WHEN HE SEES IT!
HEY!
NOOOO!
PAWS OFF THE RING, TURNER!
WAIT!
DROP IT!
PLEASE, TURNER! I FOUND IT FIRST!
NEVER!
I'M GIVING IT TO EVIL MASTER!
BOSH!
LOOK, MURPHY! A SPAGHETTI RING ON THE CEILING!
OH NO!
GOLLY, ROBERT, YOU'RE RIGHT!
WE SHOULD GIVE IT TO EVIL MASTER, HE'LL MAKE US TOP MINIONS!
GIVE ME A BOOST, ZAK!
GOT IT!
YOU ROCK, MURPHY!
NO! I'M MEANT TO GIVE IT TO EVIL MASTER!
OOPS, I DROPPED IT...
MURPHY! YOU KLUTZ!
BOING
BOING
PLOP
OOO, CONFLICT! LET'S JOIN IN!
HEY, LOOK! A SPAGHETTI RING!
SO SHINY!
OOO! EVIL MASTER WOULD BE SO HAPPY WITH WHOEVER GAVE IT TO HIM!
WELL, WELL, WELL, IF IT ISN'T MR. SMART...
DON'T EVEN THINK ABOUT IT...
TOO LATE!
CHAAARGE!
FOR EVIL MASTER!

DEALING WITH RING LOSS
NEILL, GRAB IT!
YES! GOT IT!
WAIT... I LOST IT...
OH, COME ON!
WHERE DID IT GO?!
WHAT THE...?!
IS THAT...?
I CAN'T BELIEVE MY EVIL EYES! ONE PRECIOUS SHINY SPAGHETTI RING!
I WILL CHERISH YOU FOREV—
SPLUUURGE
GAAAAAAH!
SORRY TO BARGE IN, EVIL MASTER! I FOUND A SPAGHETTI RING AND WAS GOING TO GIVE IT TO YOU, BUT—
IT'S... GONE. I ALMOST HAD IT.
IS EVERYTHING OKAY, EVIL MASTER?
SHUFFLE SHUFFLE SHUFFLE
ERRR, WE SHOULD GO...
SEEYA, EUGENE!
THIS'LL MAKE YOU FEEL BETTER, EVIL MASTER!
SING WITH ME! BING BONG BING BONG CHRISTMAAAS!

RING OF FIRE: PART 1
NUMBER 8! EUGENE! GET OVER HERE NOW!
I DO BELIEVE I HAVE DEVISED MY BEST WORLD-DOMINATION PLAN YET!
OKAY, JUST ONE LASER BEAM THERE, AND A DETACHABLE MEGA-BLASTER THERE, AAAAND...
VOILÀ!
UM, SIR... YOU'VE ONLY DRAWN RINGS...
RINGINATION!
SHRINK RINGS
HOW DARE YOU MOCK MY DRAWINGS, NUMBER 8?!
NO, SIR, I'M JUST STATING THE FACTS.
YOU'RE A FACT!
UM...NO, WAIT... WHAT?
NOW MAKE YOURSELF USEFUL AND BRING ME A BOWL OF SPAGHETTI RINGS!
WELL, THAT WAS WEIRD...
MAYBE HE'S FORGOTTEN THAT ALL THE SPAGHETTI RINGS WERE STOLEN?
WE BEST KEEP A CLOSE EYE ON HIM, EUGENE.

?
EUGENE!
WHAT ARE YOU DOING IN HERE?!
KEEPING A CLOSE EYE ON YOU, EVIL MASTER.
GET OUT! AND GO TIDY THE SPAGHETTI-RING STORAGE ROOM!
THE SPAGHETTI-RING CANS MUST BE STACKED IN ROWS OF THREE.
NUMBER 8!
GET TO THE *INRINGTION ROOM OF EVIL* NOW!
WE HAVE WORK TO DO! A RING TO DOMINATE!
I MEAN, *WORLD!*
SO, NUMBER 8, YOU NEED TO CONNECT ALL THE WIRES LIKE THIS... LIKE A RING.
I DON'T QUITE UNDERSTAND HOW THIS WORLD-DOMINATION PLAN IS GOING TO WORK BY DOING THAT, SIR.
RINGS! THAT'S HOW?! *YOU INCOMPETENT BIG RING!*
HAS ANYONE EVER TOLD YOU WHAT A FINE RING YOU'RE WEARING ON YOUR FACE?
ERM, MY *MONOCLE*, SIR?
RING, NUMBER 8. RING.
ANYWAY! BACK TO THE PLAN! WE NEED TO CONNECT THE RED RINGS TO THESE POWER RINGS...
AND THAT'S HOW THE RINGATRON 5000 WILL BE ACTIVATED.
WELL, RING ALONG, NUMBER 8! THERE'S NO TIME TO LOSE!

EUGENE, I THINK WE MAY HAVE A PROBLEM...
OOOH, EVIL MASTER HAS BEEN DRAWING MORE RINGS!
RINGS
I NEED TO DO SOME RESEARCH TO SEE IF I CAN GET TO THE BOTTOM OF HIS STRANGE BEHAVIOR.
I THOUGHT THIS BOWL OF PASTA SQUARES MIGHT HELP...
GOOD LUCK, EUGENE!
UM, EVIL MASTER...
I MADE YOU SOME LUNCH.
A NICE FRESH BOWL OF PASTA SQUARES! LOOK AT THE PRETTY GEOMETRIC SHAPES!
THESE ARE NOT SPAGHETTI RINGS!!!
SPAGHETTI RINGS DON'T HAVE CORNERS!
BOSH
BUT, EVIL MASTER, REMEMBER ALL THE SPAGHETTI RINGS WERE STOLEN BY THAT EVIL KITTY, EVILYN!
ARE YOU OKAY, EVIL MASTER?
EVIL MASTER?
WHY ARE YOU LOOKING AT ME LIKE THAT?
RINGSY RING RING?
SPAGHEEEEEEETTI RIIIIIIIIIIING!
I MUST CONSUME YOU!

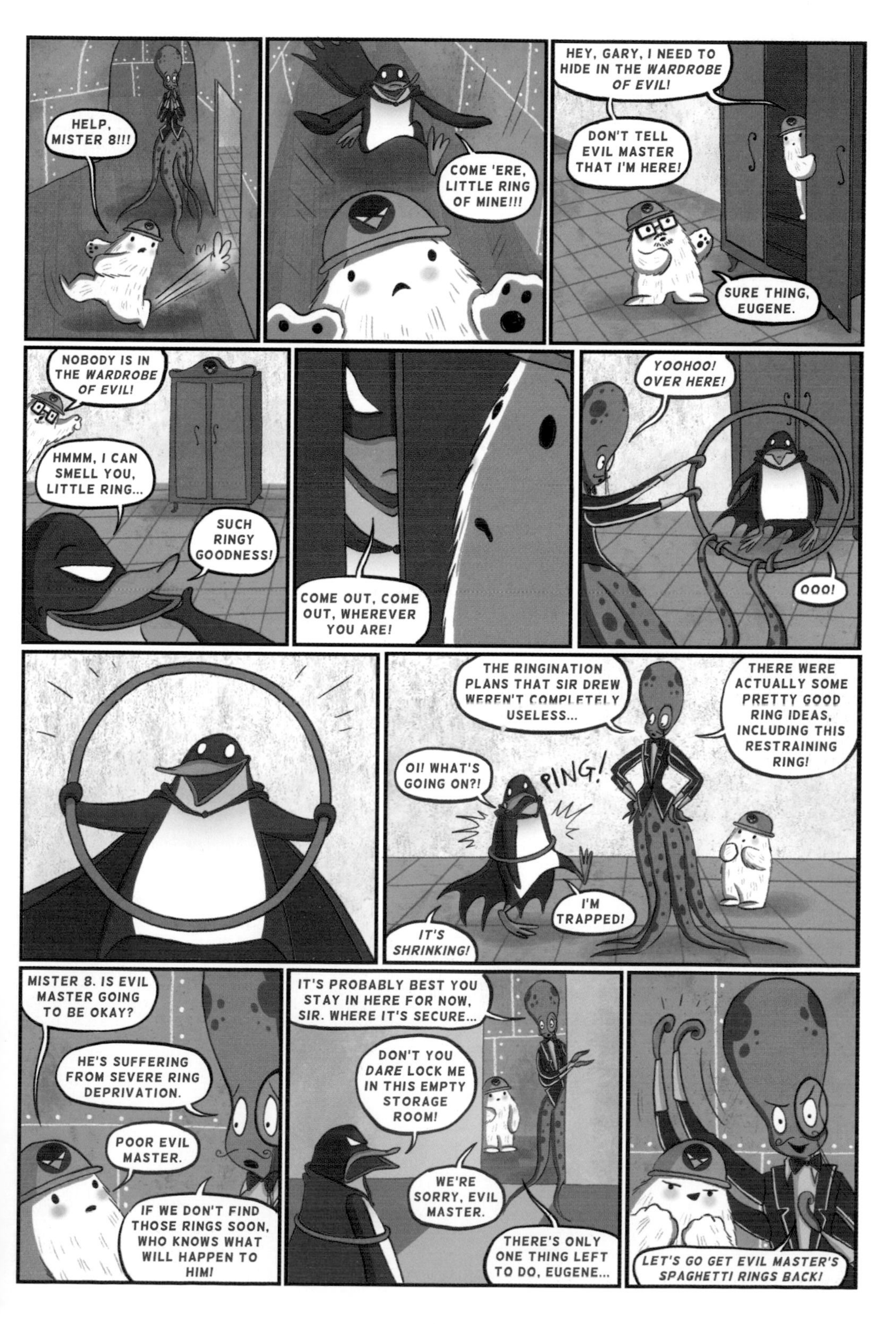
HELP, MISTER 8!!!
COME 'ERE, LITTLE RING OF MINE!!!
HEY, GARY, I NEED TO HIDE IN THE *WARDROBE OF EVIL*!
DON'T TELL EVIL MASTER THAT I'M HERE!
SURE THING, EUGENE.
NOBODY IS IN THE *WARDROBE OF EVIL*!
HMMM, I CAN SMELL YOU, LITTLE RING...
SUCH RINGY GOODNESS!
COME OUT, COME OUT, WHEREVER YOU ARE!
YOOHOO! OVER HERE!
OOO!
THE RINGINATION PLANS THAT SIR DREW WEREN'T COMPLETELY USELESS...
THERE WERE ACTUALLY SOME PRETTY GOOD RING IDEAS, INCLUDING THIS RESTRAINING RING!
OI! WHAT'S GOING ON?!
PING!
I'M TRAPPED!
IT'S SHRINKING!
MISTER 8. IS EVIL MASTER GOING TO BE OKAY?
HE'S SUFFERING FROM SEVERE RING DEPRIVATION.
POOR EVIL MASTER.
IF WE DON'T FIND THOSE RINGS SOON, WHO KNOWS WHAT WILL HAPPEN TO HIM!
IT'S PROBABLY BEST YOU STAY IN HERE FOR NOW, SIR. WHERE IT'S SECURE...
DON'T YOU *DARE* LOCK ME IN THIS EMPTY STORAGE ROOM!
WE'RE SORRY, EVIL MASTER.
THERE'S ONLY ONE THING LEFT TO DO, EUGENE...
LET'S GO GET EVIL MASTER'S SPAGHETTI RINGS BACK!

RING OF FIRE: PART 2

ANY SIGN OF THE BOTTOM, EUGENE?
AHA! WE HAVE TOUCH-DOWN!
THE CIRCULAR DETECTOR IS BUZZING LIKE CRAZY NOW!
WE MUST BE ON THE RIGHT TRACK!
OKAY, THAT WENT DARK...
THAT DEFINITELY LOOKS LIKE A TRAP...
DO NOT, UNDER ANY CIRCUMSTANCES, STEP ON *ANY* OF THOSE RINGS, EUGENE.
OKAY?
OH.
AAAAAAAAH!
BOSH!
OOF!
GASP THE SPAGHETTI RINGS!
WELL, WELL, WELL... IF IT ISN'T THE EIGHT-TENTACLED FREAK AND THE USELESS BALL OF FLUFF!
WE MEET AGAIN!

YOU'VE ARRIVED AT THE PERFECT TIME... I WAS JUST ABOUT TO END THE WORLD.
DON'T COME ANY CLOSER OR YOU WILL BE TURNED TO DUST.
NO, EVILYN! YOU CAN'T END THE WORLD!
I HAVE THE ULTIMATE DOOMSDAY WEAPON READY TO BLAST THE WORLD INTO A BAZILLION MILLION PIECES!
AND DO YOU KNOW WHAT THE PERFECT FUEL FOR MY DOOMSDAY WEAPON IS?!
SPAGHETTI RINGS!
WELL, THAT EXPLAINS WHY SHE STOLE THEM ALL, I GUESS...
THEY CONTAIN THE PERFECT RATIO OF TOMATO JUICE AND RINGINESS TO MAKE THE MACHINE EXTRA DOOMY! EEHEEHEEHEEHEEEEE!
IT WILL BE THE END OF THE WORLD AS WE KNOW IT!
WE'LL BE SAFE HERE IN MY SECRET BASE. PREPARE TO HEAR THE WORLD SHATTER ABOVE YOU!
LET'S CHANT TO MAKE IT MORE DRAMATIC!
RINGY RINGY RIIING RIIING RIIIIIING!
LET THE END OF THE WORLD COMMENCE!
IN THREE...
EEEHEEHEEHEE!
TWO!
OH NO! EVIL MASTER IS OUT THERE!
ONE!
THE END OF THE WORLD IS VERY... QUIET.
?
NOT SO FAST, COUSIN!

OI! WHAT HAVE YOU DONE TO MY DOOMSDAY WEAPON?!
WHAT DOOMSDAY WEAPON?
OH, YOU MEAN THE ONE I JUST DESTROYED?
WHAT?!
I CAN'T HAVE MY LITTLE COUSIN ENDING THE WORLD I'M MEANT TO BE TAKING OVER, EH?!
SAY HELLO TO MY NEW PEA-PEA GUN!
HEY! NO! WAIT!
YOU WILL PAY FOR THIS, COUSIN!
EVIL CAT! YOU JUST SAVED THE WORLD!
PFFFT, ONLY FOR MYSELF!
NOW, IF YOU DON'T MIND, I'M GOING TO TEST MY PEA-PEA GUN OUT ON THESE SPAGHETTI RINGS, AND THEN THE TWO OF YOU...
NOT THE SPAGHETTI RINGS!
EUGENE! CAREFUL!
HUP!
WHOOOSH
ZZZZPPP
PA-DOING!
NOOOOOOO!!!
EUGENE! THAT WAS AMAZING!
YOU SAVED ALL THE SPAGHETTI RINGS!
I'VE ALWAYS BEEN QUITE GOOD AT THROWING STUFF.
LOOKING GOOD, COUSIN!
AAAARGH!
MY HAT IS NOW A PEA, BUT I THINK IT QUITE SUITS ME, HEE HEE!
EUGENE, YOU ARE A HERO!
AND YOUR PEA-HAT LOOKS LOVELY.

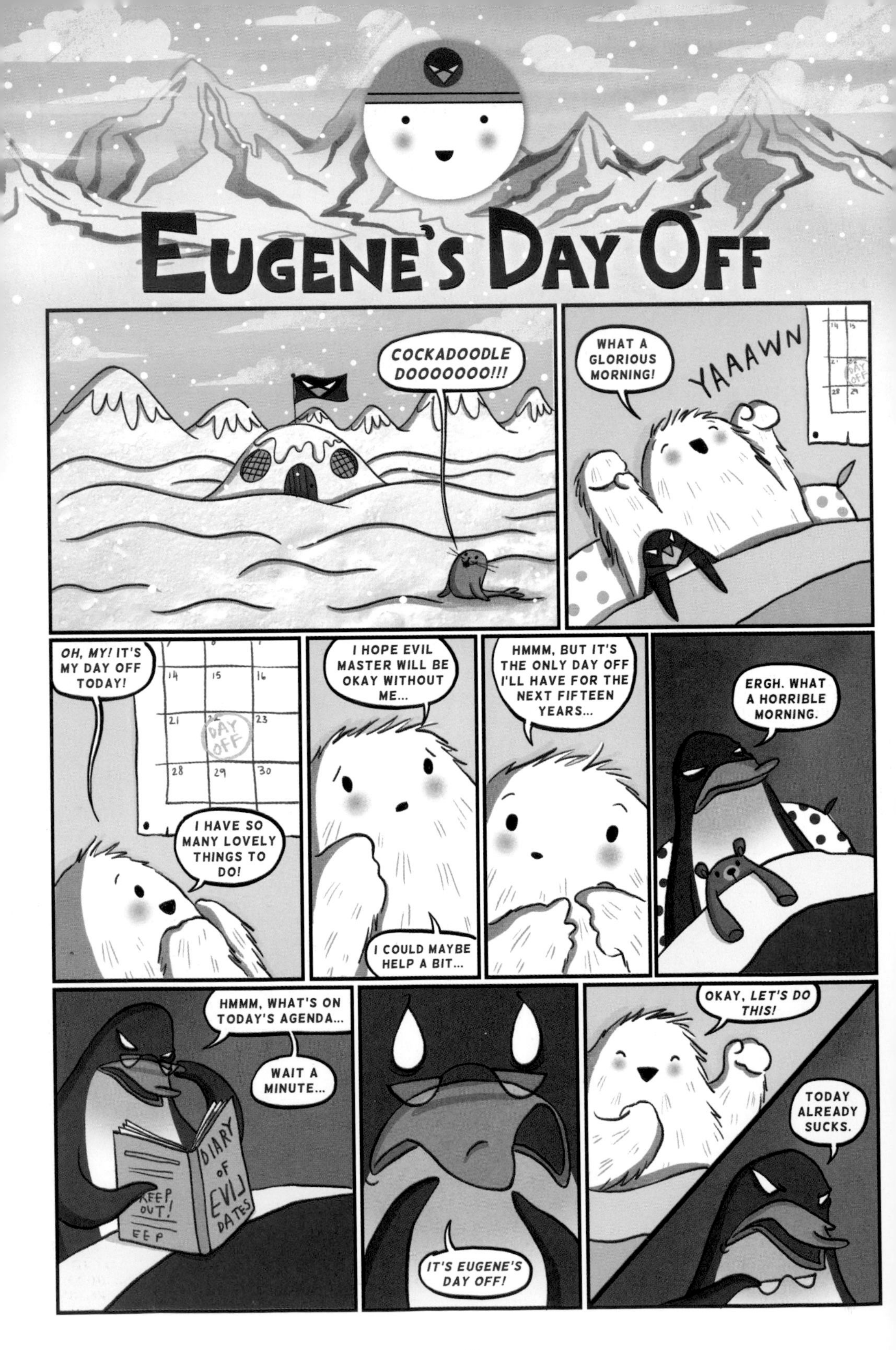
EUGENE'S DAY OFF
COCKADOODLE DOOOOOOO!!!
WHAT A GLORIOUS MORNING!
YAAAWN
DAY OFF
OH, MY! IT'S MY DAY OFF TODAY!
DAY OFF
I HAVE SO MANY LOVELY THINGS TO DO!
I HOPE EVIL MASTER WILL BE OKAY WITHOUT ME...
I COULD MAYBE HELP A BIT...
HMMM, BUT IT'S THE ONLY DAY OFF I'LL HAVE FOR THE NEXT FIFTEEN YEARS...
ERGH. WHAT A HORRIBLE MORNING.
HMMM, WHAT'S ON TODAY'S AGENDA...
WAIT A MINUTE...
DIARY of EVIL DATES
KEEP OUT!
EEP
IT'S EUGENE'S DAY OFF!
OKAY, LET'S DO THIS!
TODAY ALREADY SUCKS.

OOO, DAY OFF MEANS PANCAKES FOR BREAKFAST!
PANCAKES INITIATED
EVIL PRINTER PANCAKES ARE THE BEST.
NEILL!
WHERE'S MY BREAKFAST?!
EUGENE REQUESTED YOU AS HIS MINION REPLACEMENT FOR THE DAY... PROVE YOUR WORTH!
HERE WE GO, EVIL MASTER!
I'M SO HONORED TO BE TOP MINION FOR THE DAY!
BANG!
I THINK THE HASH BROWNS ARE READY...
THIS IS THE PERFECT TIME TO GIVE MY HAT A NICE BIG POLISH TO MAKE IT EXTRA SHINY!
POLISH OF EVIL
HMMM, IT'S "CAPE OF EVIL WASHING DAY" TODAY... I WONDER IF EVIL MASTER WILL NEED SOME HELP?
OH, SILLY ME! OF COURSE NOT!
DING!
KAA-CHING!
NEILL, WE'RE BEHIND ON TODAY'S TO-DO LIST.
HAVE YOU FINISHED WASHING MY CAPES OF EVIL YET?!
ALMOST DONE, EVIL MASTER!
TO-DO
THE'RE JUST DRYING...
IS THAT A MINION IN THE DRYER OF EVIL?
MAYBE...
TEN MINUTES LATER...
WHY ARE ALL MY CAPES TINY?!
EUGENE COLOR
I'M GOING TO DRAW A PICTURE OF MY MOST FAVORITE THINGS!
AAH, JUST PERFECT!
I THINK EVIL MASTER WILL LOVE IT!
I BET NEILL IS HAVING A WONDERFUL TIME HELPING EVIL MASTER.
I CAN'T WAIT TO START HELPING HIM AGAIN TOMORROW!

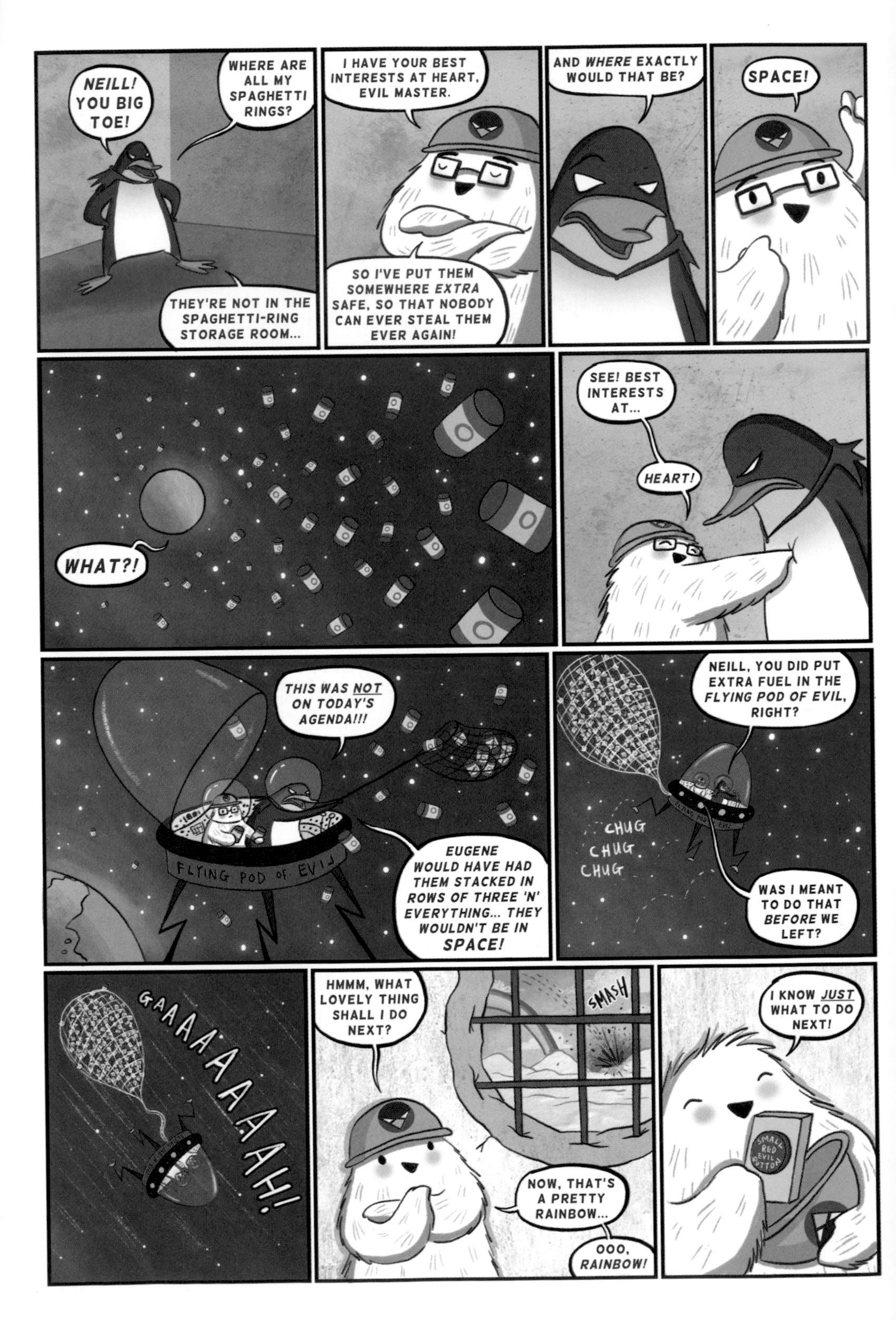
NEILL! YOU BIG TOE!
WHERE ARE ALL MY SPAGHETTI RINGS?
THEY'RE NOT IN THE SPAGHETTI-RING STORAGE ROOM...
I HAVE YOUR BEST INTERESTS AT HEART, EVIL MASTER.
SO I'VE PUT THEM SOMEWHERE EXTRA SAFE, SO THAT NOBODY CAN EVER STEAL THEM EVER AGAIN!
AND WHERE EXACTLY WOULD THAT BE?
SPACE!
WHAT?!
SEE! BEST INTERESTS AT...
HEART!
THIS WAS NOT ON TODAY'S AGENDA!!!
FLYING POD OF EVIL
EUGENE WOULD HAVE HAD THEM STACKED IN ROWS OF THREE 'N' EVERYTHING... THEY WOULDN'T BE IN SPACE!
NEILL, YOU DID PUT EXTRA FUEL IN THE FLYING POD OF EVIL, RIGHT?
CHUG CHUG CHUG
WAS I MEANT TO DO THAT BEFORE WE LEFT?
GAAAAAAAAAH!
HMMM, WHAT LOVELY THING SHALL I DO NEXT?
SMASH
NOW, THAT'S A PRETTY RAINBOW...
OOO, RAINBOW!
I KNOW JUST WHAT TO DO NEXT!
SMALL RED EVIL BUTTON

THIS IS THE PERFECT SPOT FOR A PICNIC, THANKS, KEITH!
ANY TIME, PAL!
WOULD YOU LIKE TO JOIN MY PICNIC, KEITH?
I HAVE RAINBOW COOKIES!
WELL, I CAN'T SAY NO TO A RAINBOW COOKIE!
I WONDER HOW EVIL MASTER IS DOING...
NO, NEILL, I DO NOT NEED MY OWN THEME SONG...
I WAS THINKING SOMETHING IN C MINOR... TO MAKE YOU SOUND OMINOUS.
EVIL EMPEROOOOR PENGUIIIN IS EVIIIIIL! HIS CAPE IS RED, THAT'S WHAT I SAID, OH YEEEEAH!
NEVER DO THAT AGAIN.
NOW, FOCUS!
EVIL
THIS INVENTION IS HIGHLY EXPLOSIVE, SO WE HAVE TO BE EXTRA CAREFUL UNTIL IT HAS BEEN PLANTED DEEP WITHIN THE ATLANTIC OCEAN...
SO DO NOT, UNDER ANY CIRCUMSTANCES, PULL THE RED WIRE.
OH... YOU MEAN, THIS ONE?
EVIL
I'M SURE HE'S DOING FINE WITHOUT ME.
BOOM!

On Thin Ice: Part 1

HUH?
PLANTS NEVER GROW AROUND HERE...
IT'S FAR TOO COLD FOR A LITTLE FELLOW LIKE YOU.
I'M SORRY, THAT WAS RUDE OF ME.
YOU ARE A VERY LOVELY PLANT, OF COURSE!
MY NAME IS EUGENE, AND IT'S VERY NICE TO MEET YOU.
I'M SURE YOU'LL LOVE IT AROUND HERE.
IT'S EVER SO PEACEFUL.
YOU'D GET ON WELL WITH EVIL MASTER, Y'KNOW. HE LOOKS GRUMPY, BUT HE'S REALLY RATHER WONDERFUL.
AND MISTER 8 IS THE LOVELIEST OCTOPUS IN THE WORLD.
EVIL MASTER IS GOING TO RULE THE WHOLE WORLD, YOU KNOW.
AND I KNOW HE'LL BE THE MOST WONDERFUL WORLD LEADER OF THEM ALL!
HE'S A VERY CARING PENGUIN UNDERNEATH THAT SWOOSHY RED CAPE OF HIS.
HE'S REALLY VERY—
CRACK

OH! WHAT WAS THAT NOISE?
CRACK
OH, MY!
CRACK
CRACK
OH, DEAR, I CAN'T REACH!
NO!
THAT WAS MY SPECIAL SITTING PATCH.
I DON'T UNDERSTAND. WHY IS THE GROUND BROKEN?
WELL, I GUESS IT'S JUST YOU AND ME FOR NOW, STRANGE LITTLE PLANT.

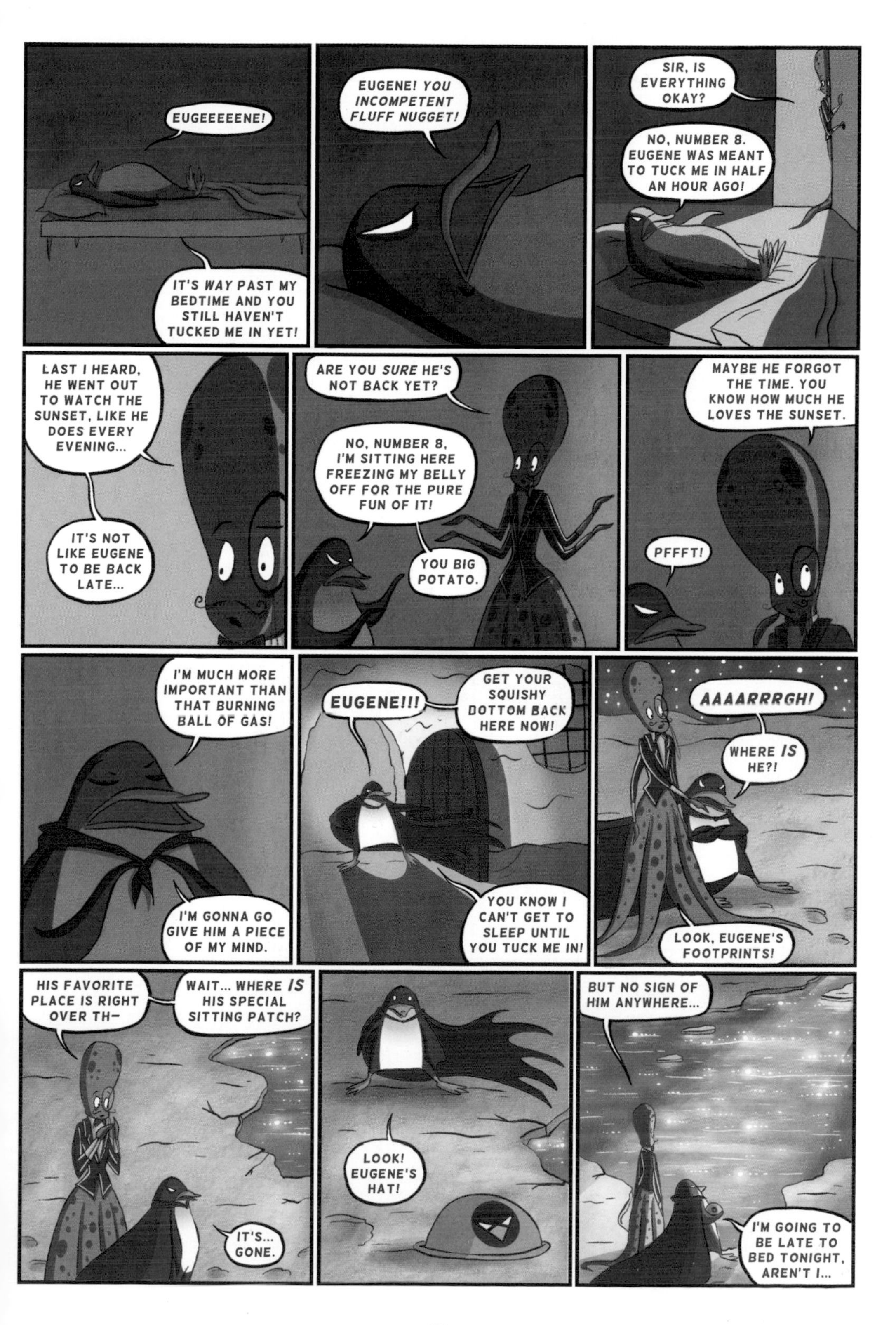
EUGEEEEENE!
IT'S WAY PAST MY BEDTIME AND YOU STILL HAVEN'T TUCKED ME IN YET!
EUGENE! YOU INCOMPETENT FLUFF NUGGET!
SIR, IS EVERYTHING OKAY?
NO, NUMBER 8. EUGENE WAS MEANT TO TUCK ME IN HALF AN HOUR AGO!
LAST I HEARD, HE WENT OUT TO WATCH THE SUNSET, LIKE HE DOES EVERY EVENING...
IT'S NOT LIKE EUGENE TO BE BACK LATE...
ARE YOU SURE HE'S NOT BACK YET?
NO, NUMBER 8, I'M SITTING HERE FREEZING MY BELLY OFF FOR THE PURE FUN OF IT!
YOU BIG POTATO.
MAYBE HE FORGOT THE TIME. YOU KNOW HOW MUCH HE LOVES THE SUNSET.
PFFFT!
I'M MUCH MORE IMPORTANT THAN THAT BURNING BALL OF GAS!
I'M GONNA GO GIVE HIM A PIECE OF MY MIND.
EUGENE!!!
GET YOUR SQUISHY BOTTOM BACK HERE NOW!
YOU KNOW I CAN'T GET TO SLEEP UNTIL YOU TUCK ME IN!
AAAARRRGH!
WHERE IS HE?!
LOOK, EUGENE'S FOOTPRINTS!
HIS FAVORITE PLACE IS RIGHT OVER TH—
WAIT... WHERE IS HIS SPECIAL SITTING PATCH?
IT'S... GONE.
LOOK! EUGENE'S HAT!
BUT NO SIGN OF HIM ANYWHERE...
I'M GOING TO BE LATE TO BED TONIGHT, AREN'T I...

ON THIN ICE: PART 2

WELL, THIS IS HIGHLY INCONVENIENT.
WE NEED TO FIND EUGENE BEFORE HE GETS TOO FAR AWAY, SIR.
YES, BUT HOW?!
LET'S USE THE "SUBMARINE OF EVIL" I BUILT FOR YOU...
NOPE, IT SANK.
WHAT?! HOW?
I SANK IT.
WHY?!
I DIDN'T LIKE THE COLOR.
STOP WASTING MY TIME, NUMBER 8, WE MUST THINK FAST!
WHAT WAS THAT?!
BLOP
IT'S THE SMALL RED EVIL BUTTON!
REMEMBER, EUGENE ALWAYS KEEPS IT IN HIS HAT!
SIR, THIS IS IT! THIS IS THE KEY TO FINDING EUGENE!
WHAT DO YOU MEAN... THE "KEY"?
OH... HOLY BANANAS, NO. JUST NO...
THERE MUST BE ANOTHER WAY!
WELL, WELL... I DIDN'T EXPECT YOUR TWO HANDSOME FACES TO BE AT THE OTHER END WHEN I GOT THE RED ALERT!
I WOULD'VE MADE MORE SPARKLE.
I CAN'T BELIEVE THIS IS HAPPENING...
BUT IF IT MEANS FINDING EUGENE... I GUESS I'LL COPE.
LET'S GO FIND THAT LOVELY EUGENE!
JUST NEED TO TAKE A DETOUR TO THE RAINBOW REFILL STATION.
WON'T TAKE A MINUTE.
IT'LL BE A BUMPY RIDE THERE THOUGH. SORRY!
RAINBOW REFILLS HERE...
FREE EXTRA SPARKLES EVERY MONDAY
NO CO2 EMISSIONS
CLEAN SPARKLY FUEL
EXTRA SPARKLE MONDAY! IT'S YOUR LUCKY DAY, GUYS!
IS IT? IS IT REALLY?
OH, EUGENE, WHERE ARE YOU?! SAVE ME FROM THIS ONE-HORNED RAINBOW MACHINE!

OH, DEAR...
I HOPE NO MORE ICE BREAKS... I CAN'T SWIM.
CRACK
CRACK
AT LEAST I HAVE YOU, LITTLE PLANT.
OH, MY!
CRACK
CRACK
OH, DEAR, THIS ISN'T GOOD!
OH, I DON'T KNOW WHAT TO DO, LITTLE PLANT...
CRACK
CRACK
CRACK
IF IT BREAKS ANY MORE, WE'LL FALL IN!
CRACK
AAAAAH!
HELP!

HEY, EUGENE, YOU OKAY, LITTLE DUDE?
HUH?
KEITH?
HOW DID YOU FIND ME?
IF IT WASN'T FOR THE LITTLE GREEN THING FLOATING ON THE WATER, WE'D NEVER HAVE FOUND YOU!
TRYING TO SPOT A TINY WHITE MINION AMONGST ALL THE ICE AND WATER ISN'T EASY!
OH, LITTLE PLANT!
YOU HELPED ME!
C'MON, LET'S TAKE YOU TO EEP AND OCTO-MAN... I LEFT THEM ON A RAINBOW.
EUGENE!
OH, I'M SO GLAD TO SEE YOU AGAIN, EVIL MASTER.
YES, WELL, DON'T EXPECT ME TO BE TOO PLEASED.... YOU'RE EXTREMELY LATE FOR TUCKING ME IN TO BED.
YOU'RE THE ONLY ONE WHO MAKES IT EXTRA COMFY.

ESSENCE OF EUGENE
NUMBER 8, I CAN'T HELP FEELING LIKE THERE'S SOMETHING IMPORTANT HAPPENING TODAY...
WELL, SIR, IT'S EUGENE'S—
GAH! IT'S PROBABLY SOMETHING I ATE.
BUT, SIR—
HUSH, SQUID.
I HAVE JUST FINISHED PLOTTING MY NEW ACTION-PACKED PLAN FOR WORLD DOMINATION!
AND THE KEY TO MY SUCCESS WILL BE...
CANDLES!
CANDLES, SIR?
SOUNDS EVER SO... ACTION-PACKED.
ARE YOU MOCKING ME, NUMBER 8?
I WOULDN'T DREAM OF IT, SIR. *COUGH*
THOSE HUMANS LOVE A SCENTED CANDLE, ESPECIALLY WHEN IT SMELLS LIKE CHRISTMAS OR FAIRIES 'N' STUFF.
SO I HAVE CREATED MY OWN RANGE OF SCENTED CANDLES CALLED "CANDLES THAT SMELL LIKE STUFF"...
AND HOW EXACTLY WILL THESE CANDLES HELP YOU TO TAKE OVER THE WORLD, SIR?
THAT'S THE AWESOME PART, NUMBER 8. WHEN THE CANDLE IS LIT, IT'LL GIVE OFF A SCENT OF ULTIMATE EVIL!!!
AND THEY'LL BE HYPNOTIZED TO THINK ABOUT AND WORSHIP ONLY ME!

I MADE THE CANDLES SMELL GOOD BY ADDING A SAMPLE OF EUGENE'S FUR TO THE CANDLE MIX...
BUT REALLY THAT JUST COVERS UP THE PUNGENT AROMA OF ULTIMATE EVIL!
NOW, WATCH THE AD I MADE, NUMBER 8.
IT'S THE BEST THING YOU'LL EVER SEE.
ARE YOU BORED OF YOUR BORING CANDLES?!
OH, MY...
WELL, LOOK NO FURTHER!
"CANDLES THAT SMELL LIKE STUFF!"
KAACHING!
THESE ARE THE BEST CANDLES YOU'LL EVER SMELL, BECAUSE...
THEY SMELL LIKE STUFF!
HMMMMMM
SO PURCHASE YOURS FOR JUST
$3.99 PER CANDLE AT
WWW.EVILCANDLES.COM
YEAH!
AND THAT'S NOT ALL...
THERE ARE THREE FLAVORS TO CHOOSE FROM:
WORLD LEADER
SQUID
AND
EUGENE!
CANDLES THAT SMELL LIKE STUFF!
BUY ONE OR ELSE
I DON'T KNOW WHAT TO SAY...
THERE ARE NO WORDS FOR THE LEVEL OF AWESOME YOU JUST WITNESSED.
PING!
NEW EVIL-MAIL RECEIVED
OOO! MY FIRST CANDLE SALE! IT'S WORKING!!!

PREPARE YOURSELVES, PATHETIC HUMAN BEINGS... *TO FIND OUT WHAT ULTIMATE EVIL SMELLS LIKE!*
THE SALES ARE SOARING, NUMBER 8...
SOON ENOUGH THEY'LL BE DREAMING ONLY OF ME!
JUST AS SOON AS THEY LIGHT THOSE CANDLES!
MEANWHILE...
EUGENE IS SO DREAMY!
EUGENE IS MY SPIRIT ANIMAL!
I LOVE EUGENE MORE THAN MY TAIL!
I LOVE EUGENE MORE THAN MY BICEPS!
EUGENE.
THAT IS ALL.
ALL HAIL EUGENE!
EUGENE IS AMAZING!
THE BEST!
I LOVE EUGENE!
KING!
EUGENE RULES!
RAINBOWS AND LOVELY THINGS!

WE LOVE EUGENE!
EEP HQ
NUMBER 8, DID YOU HEAR SOMETHING?
UM, SIR... YOU MIGHT WANT TO SEE THIS.
IT APPEARS YOUR CANDLES ARE WORKING...
BREAKING NEWS
JUST NOT IN THE WAY YOU INTENDED.
IT APPEARS THE WORLD HAS GONE CRAZY FOR EUGENE. AND WHO CAN BLAME THEM?! HE'S THE BEST!!!
EUGENE SHOULD TOTALLY RULE, RIGHT?! ALL I CAN THINK ABOUT IS HOW WONDERFUL AND CUTE AND FLUFFY EUGENE IS! EUGENE RULES THE WORLD!!!
BREAKING NEWS
EUGENE
EUGENE RULES!
WE ♥ EUGENE!
ALL HAIL EUGENE
EUGENE FEVER!
WHAT?!
THEY'RE INHALING ESSENCE OF EVIL!!!
WHY ARE THEY WORSHIPPING EUGENE?!
IT SEEMS WHEN YOU ADDED EUGENE'S FUR, THE ESSENCE OF EUGENE OVERRIDES ANY OUNCE OF EVIL PRESENT IN THE CANDLE...
HE'S JUST TOO CUTE AND CUDDLY...
SO, IN EFFECT, SIR...
EUGENE HAS TAKEN OVER THE WORLD.
OH, YAY! THIS IS THE BEST BIRTHDAY EVER!